DAGON

DAGON

FRED CHAPPELL

LOUISIANA STATE UNIVERSITY PRESS
BATON ROUGE

Copyright © 1987 by Fred Chappell. From THE FRED CHAPPELL
    READER by Fred Chappell. Reprinted by arrangement with St. Mar-
    tin's Press, LLC.
Originally published by Harcourt, Brace & World, Inc.
LSU Press edition published 2002
All rights reserved
Manufactured in the United States of America

11 10 09 08 07 06 05 04 03 02
5 4 3 2 1

Pieces of this book first appeared in *Carolina Quarterly* and *Red Clay Reader*.

Library of Congress Cataloging-in-Publication Data

Chappell, Fred, 1936–
    Dagon / Fred Chappell.
        p. cm. — (Voices of the South)
    ISBN 0-8071-2791-4 (alk. paper)
        1. Inheritance and succession—Fiction. 2. Fertility Cults—Fiction.
    3. North Carolina—Fiction. 4. Authorship—Fiction. 5. Farm life—Fiction.
    6. Clergy—Fiction. I. Title. II. Series.

PS3553.H298 D34 2002
813'.54—dc21

                                                            2001054903

The paper in this book meets the guidelines for permanence and durability
of the Committee on Production Guidelines for Book Longevity of the
Council on Library Resources. ∞

Dedicated to the George Garretts
and to the Peter Taylors
and to the memory of Richard McKenna

Ph'nglui mglw'nafh Cthulhu R'lyeh wgah'nagl fhtagn.

I

ONE

About 9:30 the next morning he entered the downstairs room which faced the almost painfully blue west and the tall ridge across the little valley, the room which his grandparents had used to call the "sun parlor." He advanced into the room a way and halted, seeming to feel the whole fabric of the house tremulous with his footsteps. And he had paused to consider, well, to think about how much there actually *was* to consider. The onus of inheritance was already beginning to rub a bit. —The room was familiarly musty and the two windows, eyed and wavy, were decent in their gray gauzy curtains. Over the bisected window in the door which opened to the outside, the glass curtain was stretched tight with rods at top and bottom so that the cloth was pulled into stiff ribs, stiff as fingers of the dead. He took another step and again hesitated, hearing the quiet wary rattle of glassware somewhere. Meditating, he shifted his weight forward and back, rocking on the balls of his feet. Had all the floor timbers melted away with dry rot? He couldn't quite bring himself to doubt, staring down frowning at the regular lines of dark oak flooring, board laid solid by board. Even the layer of dust which was spread like cheesecloth about his feet didn't entirely dull the hard polish of the wood. He disliked thinking of these careful rows ripped up, exposing the broad rough subflooring; and then that too taken away to get at the flaking bones of the house. But there was probably no preventing it. He sighed, and as he inhaled, agitated atoms of dust pierced his nostrils brightly. Twice he sneezed, and rubbed his nose roundly with his wrist, squeezed his eyebrows in his palm. Had he really heard an echo to his sneeze? The room hardly seemed large enough to give up echoes—it was about twenty feet square with a high ceiling—but it was a room truly made for secondary presences, for reverberations. This wasn't the whole room. Opposite him, double doors, divided into small glass rectangles, closed off what was actually the remainder of this room. In the left door his image stood, hand still over his face, and he was all cut into pieces in the panes. He dropped his pale hand to his side, and in the glass the movement coruscated.

He moved toward the west wall and once again his image, larger now and darker, accosted him. His head and torso stood before him, sliced now into the pattern of an oval enclosed in roundish triangles and seemingly stacked in the shelves of the dark old writing cabinet. He shrugged, turned away. The low sofa, piled with fancy pillows and cushions, sat stolid against the

4

opposite wall. The obese horror was draped over with a picture rug, but it was easy enough to guess how it was: covered with a vinous prickly nap and with three huge cushions laid on the springs. The wool picture rug had two fringes of red tassel and displayed a Levantine scene: in the market place the wine seller sits comfortably beneath his awning while the dark and turbaned stranger looms above him on his camel, and behind in the dusty street the woman returns from the well, her water jug shouldered. This tableau splotched with a profusion of pillows and cushions, green, red, yellow, gaudy flowers, knowing birds, birds darkly wise. In the center of the sofa were two oblong companion pillows, shouldered so closely together that they looked like the Decalogue tablets. They were white, or had been white, and painfully stitched upon them with blue thread were companion mottoes, companion pictures. In the left pillow lies a girl, her long blue hair asprawl about her face, her eyes innocently shut, asleep. The motto: I SLEPT AND DREAMED THAT LIFE WAS BEAUTY. But the story continued, and on the next pillow her innocence is all torn away: there she stands, gripping a round broom; her hair now is pinned up severely and behind her sits a disheartening barrel churn. I WOKE AND FOUND THAT LIFE WAS DUTY. The pillows sat, stuffed and stiff as disapproving bishops; they could, he thought, serve as twin tombstones for whole gray generations. It was in no way difficult to imagine the fingers of his grandmother, tough and knobbly, wearily working upon these wearying legends, these most speaking epitaphs. It was more discouraging still to wonder if perhaps this task hadn't been performed by his grandmother's mother. Even without thinking he doubted that there was anything in his blood which could now fight back to that bitter use of mind; he just wasn't so tough. . . . No; no, that wasn't true, either. Slow, wet, easy living hadn't got to his Puritan core, not *really*. He *could* hump logs together to make a house; *he* could plow the long furrow as straight as a killing arrow. It was simply that he didn't have to: the world had got easier, even the sky. All that temper was still in him and not really very hidden, and it was no strange matter that these two pillows could cause to rise in his mind narrow visions of those stringent decades. He could see his male ancestry as grainy and rough as if they had all been hacked from stone. They didn't drink, didn't smoke; they didn't read, and all books other than the great black one were efficient instruments of Sathanas. The only fun they had was what he was living evidence of. —And very probably not.— He could imagine them, his whiskery forefathers, stalking wifeward to beget, stolid, unmoved as men readying themselves to slaughter hogs. And some hint of that too. The women were no better. Their hands were pained knots, like blighted unopenable buds. Their eyes were stuffed with the opaque ice which had clenched over the fear of their hearts. . . . And yet, and yet there was always something faintly comforting in thinking upon the gelid principles with which his grandfathers had shored up themselves for duty, military or familial, or for the rich farming business.

He was vaguely bothered, nettled, and he turned away from contemplating the pillows. Across from him was the wide entry to a dark formal dining room, and in the near corner a complacent fat club chair. He turned round and round, feeling the windows slide over his sight and the serrated glitter of the glass doors, and found himself, in a momentary accident, face to face with the wall. It was plaster, and he could discern in its grain the sweep of the maker's trowel and swirled signs of the hair. In the morning silence the wall seemed as vocal as everything else in the room. Illumination, a gilt tin contraption which sported naked light bulbs, hung suspended from the ceiling by a gilt chain, and a thick webby electric cord sidled through the links. Before the piled sofa sat a low table, the wood mahogany-stained, with a glass top which displayed photographs that could dim, but not curl, with age: four rows of gray-and-black squares, instants of frozen miming that he would not examine. More gilt, on the wall above the sofa: a rectangular frame which enclosed a photograph in anemic—"tinted"—colors, the faces of his grandfather and grandmother. Both the progenitors seemed masked for the picture, as severe as if they had plotted beforehand to judge the photographer, to sentence him to a life of hard labor. The eyes of the grandfather were frigid blue, the color of the windwashed March sky reflected in the ice of a puddle. Somehow the tinting process, whatever it was, had made those eyes inviting targets for wishful darts. Set jaws, assured noses, ears which would admit only acquiescent sounds. The eyes of the grandmother were gray and, though doubtless resolute, the gaze was not so personally stationed. In her clear forehead and in the rather distant aiming of her eyes there was not so much of her husband's belligerent certainty; there was a hint of troubled—but still (he had to admit it)—unshaken humanity. But it was an unyielding countenance, and he found himself brushing his hand over his face as if he had just walked through a cobweb. Awkwardly he stepped back, as though he could retreat from his unrealized action or, rather, from whatever vague thought had inspired it. Nor was he delighted to see his mind so often turning upon himself.

He pawed a mass of pillows heavily aside and sat down on the sofa; fumbled in his shirt pocket for a cigarette. The odor of the sofa submerged him; it wasn't sour exactly, but rather sweet-and-sour, palpable; musty, of course, but with an aura of times past so striking as almost to give an impression of freshness. The smell betokened what? Voluminous clothes kept with a sachet too old, so that its power had disappeared into the cloth. Or long dutiful Sunday afternoons spent with the Methodist preacher over a box of stale chocolate candies. Or dripping afternoon funerals set up in this room and garnished with flowers which had very recently given up their sickly ghosts. His spirit seemed drowning in the smell of the sofa, in the swift flood of pastness it poured out. He lit the cigarette and sucked the smoke deep, as if protecting himself, almost in fact as if smoking was an act of defiance toward the past. The smoke rose slowly, the lax strands of it parting and hanging almost motionless in the air, seemingly very solid. It was himself, in fact, who seemed flimsy; even his body, whose weight the hard sofa barely accepted, felt vaporous, tenuous: there was not enough real event attached to it to force it to existence. The room was so silent that he could hear his chest rasp against the cloth of his shirt as he breathed, and for one scary moment he imagined that this sound became increasingly faint, was dying away. He dropped the blackened paper match into a silly little ashtray, a tiny china circle with—again—gilt lines and in the center an ugly pink rose. The dead match lay across the face of the rose like a disastrous scar, and he noted it with a twinge of guilty triumph; so that almost reflexively he mashed the new cigarette into the flower, leaving there a raw streak of black ash. The small coals died immediately.

He rose and crossed the room. As he had suspected, the desk section of the dark secretary was locked, but through the glass cabinet doors he saw the small brass key lying on the middle shelf. The lock was reluctant, but the section did at last let down, exposing an interior less musty than he had imagined. There were half a dozen tight-ranked drawers and a number of bulging pigeonholes. Letters, photographs, books of check stubs, a bottle in which the ink had dried to a circular black scab, a Waterman pen with a discolored yellow nib.

He pulled from one of the pigeonholes a resisting envelope and shook the letter from it. The cheap paper had darkened with dust and the recalcitrant words had been formed with blunt pencil strokes, gray on gray. He held the sheet above his head and turned his back to the window. The words came dimly to his eyes: . . . *guess Jasper's note will be alright anyway for this yr and can renew with confidance, I guess in the neighborhood of 1500*. It would of course be concerned with money. He let it drop unfluttering and wiped his fingers on his trousers leg. From a closed drawer peeped the shiny corner of a snapshot, which he slipped out without opening the drawer. At first he couldn't comprehend what object was pictured, but it was, after all, merely an automobile, a Dodge or a Plymouth of the late '30's, black, hardily at repose before the immaculately vertical lines of a walnut tree. Why this photograph? He stared at it as if it were an urgent but indecipherable message, intently personal. The car was not new, had not been photographed on that account. It was perhaps no more than the thoughtless effort to finish up a roll of film so that a brother with his arm about the shoulders of an aunt or a wide-eyed distressed baby cousin might sooner see the light of day in their own white-edged squares. Yet here it was, the car, as bluntly and totally itself as if it had been invented for the purpose of perplexing. He tried to slide the snapshot back through the crack in the top of the drawer, but it encountered a hidden tightness and folded up, the brittle surface suddenly webbed with fine lines like a cracked china plate.

He desisted, and let the picture loll out of the front of the desk like an idiot untasting tongue. When he once more glimpsed his darkly reflected face in the cabinet doors, his eyes looked fearful.

He turned again to the panes of glass in the double doors, this time erasing his features by bringing his face directly against one of the panes. He cupped his hands, extending them from his temples as if he were trying to see for a long distance through blinding sunlight. The interior of this room swam forward to meet him. Although there was a row of windows in the opposite wall, they were darkened by a shaggy row of fir bushes growing by the outside wall, so that this room was even dimmer than the one in which he was standing.

When he tried the knob the lock uttered an unnerving scrape, but the right-hand door swung inward easily enough. Here was real mustiness, an odor so stuffed with unmoving time that it seemed strange the pressure of it hadn't burst the doors and windows. Entering, he left unclear tracks in the dust behind him, and the dust muted his footsteps, seemed to adhere like cobweb to his shoes. The dust seemed a huge powdery cobweb. A long low comfortless-looking lounge was pushed against the wall, and the tough ornate wood of the back of it jammed into the window sill. This sofa was undraped, but the upholstery was decorated with looping broad arabesques which suggested a badly stylized jungle. There were four identical knickknack tables on thin legs; they were cluttered with more of the tiny uninviting ashtrays and with a number of small pale wooden boxes. Against the east wall sat a black upright piano which somehow seemed sagging. He crossed to it and opened it. The keys were discolored, yellowish, cracked, and in some cases the ivory was missing almost completely. He punched gingerly at middle A, then experimented with a simple triad. Middle C sounded merely a dull thump; the E and A keys produced a dissonance. No doubt the strings had rusted, the whole guts of the instrument diseased and disordered. Again he wiped his fingers on his trousers, trying to wipe away that dust which seemed to seep into the pores of his skin. With his cold hand he brushed his face too, and the back of his neck. Over the top of the piano drooped a big elaborately embroidered doily; it looked like a fishnet, a fantastic net to catch—what? Oh, whatever inhabited the surcharged air of this room. Even after he backed away from the instrument, that acrid chord seemed to hang still in his hearing; it was as if he had written indelible curse words upon something which was supposed to remain sacredly blank. He raised and dropped his shoulders in a sigh; he felt almost as if he had been working away in hard physical labor; he had never before felt his will to be so ringed about, so much at bay. Never before had he realized so acutely the invalidity of his desires, how they could be so easily canceled, simply marked out, by the impersonal presence of something, a place, an object, anything vehemently and uncaringly itself. . . . But the pastness which these two rooms (really, one room divided) enclosed was not simply the impersonal weight of dead personality but a willful belligerence, active hostility. Standing still in the center of the first room, he felt the floor stirring faintly beneath his feet, and he was convinced that the house was gathering its muscles to do him harm; it was going to spring. But then he heard the sharp-heeled footsteps which caused the quivering, and then Sheila, his blond pale pretty wife, stuck her head through the hall door.

"Come on outside, Peter," she said. "Come away."

TWO

"I didn't have the faintest idea it was even near lunch-time," he said. Standing out here under the shiny June sky, he felt perfectly at ease to stretch his arms and shoulder muscles, as if he had just awakened from a dreary, unrefreshing sleep. He opened his mouth, tasting the bright air. It was warm; he hadn't realized how cold he had become in the house. Not far away he could hear a bird singing unstintingly, pure filigree of sound. "Here," he said. "Let me take that." He lifted the big wicker basket from his wife's strained hand. "Where are we going?"

Her voice was clear and easy as water. "It's your farm; you tell me. Where is the best place on this magnificent estate to have a picnic?"

"I don't know any more about the place than you do. But maybe we'd better not go too far. They're liable to deliver our stuff today."

Sheila looked at Peter with a secret eye: her tall gangly husband, all bones and corners his body was, had already begun worrying himself. The "stuff" which was to come was mostly books and notebooks and cryptic files of index cards. Already he was concerned about finishing his book—he called it his "study"—in time. They still had about twenty-five hundred dollars left of the amount they had allowed themselves and now this nice quiet place to work, this farm willed to him by his grandparents, had dropped into their laps, and still he was worrying himself. In this warmly glowing landscape his eyes were turned inward. As they went through the sparse front lawn of the house she broke a tall stalk of plaintain off at the top and put the oozy stem end into her mouth.

He swung the basket unrhythmically as he walked. His height and boniness made him seem loping. When they came to the reddish-yellow dirt road which ran northward past the house, he hesitated. "Now which way?" he said. "We can go either way here and still be in our own domain."

It was true. The big ugly house sat almost in the center of the wide farm, the four hundred acres shaped vaguely like an open hand. It sat among smooth hills, so that if they went very far in any direction they would have to climb.

"Your wish is my command," she said.

"Well . . ." He gave her a look. Lightness and irony more or less sweet, that was Sheila. He shrugged a shoulder and started toward their car, the old blue Buick parked in the sloping driveway behind the house.

"But let's *do* walk," she said. "It's a warm lovely day,

15

and walking won't take so terribly much time. It'll be soon enough you're back to your nasty old books and note cards. Surely we're not here just for you to work."

"Still, that's mostly why we're here. At least, I hope it is." But he gave over anyway, and turning suddenly to her took her hand.

As quickly, involuntarily, she almost drew away. His hand on hers was dry and cool, actually cold, and startling in the warm sunlight. "You'll have to get used to walking," she said. "Now that you're in the country, you'll have to do all sorts of rustic things. You'll have to drink fresh milk and rob the honeybees and eat wild flowers. You're going to become a happy child of nature. I'm sure you'll make a great success of it."

"Oh, that's me. A happy child of nature."

In a hundred yards or so the road had climbed, cutting along the side of the hill. A slow dark stream ran in the narrow bottom field below; serpentine, sluggish, it reflected no light through the tall weeds and bushes that crowded to its edges. Sheila pointed toward it. "Maybe we could spread our blanket by the creek down there," she said. "It looks so nice and cool."

"Do you really want to go crawling through those weeds? I bet the whole field is full of snakes and spiders. And the ground down there'll be wet, so close to the stream."

"Weeds won't hurt you," she said. She patted the smooth leg of her pink cotton slacks. "Come on, chicken heart, it'll be very nice, bet you a pretty." She tugged at his hand, drew him to the side of the road.

"Hold on a minute." He shifted the basket to his other hand, and his body tilted perceptibly with the weight. "What in the world did you put in here, anyway? Heavy as lead."

"All kinds of surprises," she said. "Lead hamburgers, lead rolls, lead mustard . . ."

They got through the field without much difficulty and she was right, here by the stream it was cool. They found a circle of long cool grass, almost free of weeds, and shadowed by a stand of scrubby willow bushes. Sheila wafted a blue tablecloth over the ground and crawled over it on hands and knees to smooth it out. Then she stood and fingered her fine blond hair back from her temples. "Oh, this is lovely." She looked at him, an anxious inquiry. "Isn't it lovely?" The stream lapped intermittently at the banks, the dark water moved slow and dreamy through the shadows; now and again it splashed up a wink of reflected sunlight. Her face gleamed momentarily in a pure reflection of the sun. "We ought to take all our meals down here."

"Not me," he said. "I'm not getting out of bed and wallow through weeds and mud for breakfast."

"No, not breakfast. You don't have to be silly about it." She laughed. She began taking paper plates from the basket: held one up and flourished it ruefully. "These really ought to be very fine china," she said. "I've decided that we're celebrating."

"If those had been china, I'd never have got here with the basket."

She produced a large brown paper bag and drew a

17

pretty baked hen from it. "Voilà!" And there was wine too, a California white wine in a green bottle with a red foil wrapping over the top. And a mixed salad tied up in a little plastic bag. "The plates are just for the salad, anyway. You'll have to be a child of nature and eat the chicken with your own crude hands. And look: I bought some ready-made dressing." She held up a small bottle and began shaking it furiously.

He had been staring at her, awestruck. "Where did you get all this stuff? The chicken and everything. . . . What is it we're supposed to be celebrating?"

"There's a little old restaurant in the town. They were just delighted to sell me a nice baked chicken. See —while you were mooning around the house all morning I kept myself busy, planning and preparing these nice things for us. Everything just to make you happy."

He sighed. "And what is it we're celebrating?"

"Our vacation. . . . Or just being here in this good cool spot by the water. Or anything. Why not?"

"Mmnh." Descending tone of regret. He felt that he had so much yet to do that even to be happy for the opportunity would be in some way to harm it, to jinx the chance for finishing.

"Anything, we're celebrating anything you like. *Remnant Pagan Forces in American Puritanism.*"

"A bit prematurely, perhaps." He cut his words short, isolated each of them with brief pauses. He couldn't help it.

She pouted. "Now please don't be a grouch. If you begin now, you'll just be a grouch all summer and neither of us will have a good time, and you won't get any more work done than if you'd been cheerful."

"Sorry," he said. But still the word was clipped.

"Look now . . ." She leaned carefully from her kneeling position, carefully across the spread tablecloth and pulled his ear lobe. "Eat. Drink. Enjoy. Relax. Nothing bad has happened, and nothing bad is going to happen. . . . And look what I got for you for after lunch." She fumbled in the basket for a moment and took out a fat masculine cigar. "If you don't like it, I'll strangle you," she said. "It was the most expensive one they had."

Finally he relented, or at least his body did; he threw himself back on the grass and laughed. Sunlight spotted his chest and face, spots like shiny yellow eyes.

She was laughing too, a liquid twittering, but suddenly stopped. "I hope you're not laughing at me," she said. She blinked her eyes wide.

He only laughed the harder, laughing at both of them, laughing most of all at the hard core of stodginess in himself that he was afraid of. Unresting shadows poured down his throat, leaf shadows twinkled on his face.

"Oh, you *are*." She was going to become angry. She looked about for something to throw at his convulsed thin chest.

"I'm not laughing at you." He lifted his hand, smiled at her. "No, really, I'm not. . . . But you're too much for me. You're simply too much."

"Yes, that's right. You're a happy child of nature.

19

Simple. Pure. You can't understand my sophisticated complexity." She dumped salad from the moist plastic bag onto a paper plate. "Here, nature boy, eat. . . . You're an animal."

"In a lot of ways, that's true," he said, his voice taking an unconsciously serious edge. "I am simple, and you are pretty sophisticated. Anyway, you understand both of us better than I understand myself."

She took the wine bottle, peeled away the foil, unscrewed the top and poured. "Here," she said. "Drink this down and shut up. You'll give me a headache with all that psychological talk."

He hushed and they ate in silence. He kept looking at her, at her cool blond hair so spattered with light and shadow, at the way she moved her hands so freely, at the whiteness of her throat. So pretty she was, small and womanly, clear-eyed; it was a catch in his breathing. Her emotions were so mobile—she felt and responded to the slightest movement of things about her immediately and without hindrance—that he often forgot the chromium-bright hard mind which shone in the center. She was, after all, possessed of a nice intellect, superior perhaps to his own. In the core of his throat he breathed a wistful sigh, still looking. She colored slightly under his fixed gaze, she had misinterpreted it. Ho-ho-ho: so that was the drift of the breeze, was it? Her careful picnic was really a praeludium to the unaccustomed joy of making love in the open air. "In sight of God and everybody." He leaned back and got out his handkerchief and wiped at his fingers all runny with the juices of the bird. He smiled a slight dark smile.

She moved again, looked away; grew fretful under his stare. "Well, what is it then?" she said. "Do you see something you haven't seen before?"

He grinned, picked up the waxed paper cup and held it toward her. "Let's have another drink."

She mimed drawing away. "I don't know," she said. "Maybe you've had enough already. Maybe too much. You've already got staring drunk." She poured the cup full.

"That's the way, baby," he said. "Lay it on me."

She put down the bottle and flung a chicken bone at him. He sprang at her—the motion exaggerated, sudden —caught her shoulder and tumbled her over. She almost wiggled loose, but he caught her forearm and held her. She tugged as hard as she could; her face was hot and scarlet. They rolled wildly over and over in the grasses and tablecloth. Finally she got his shoulder under a pink-clad knee and held him pinned fast on one side. Her voice took a hoarse false edge. "You idiot."

"Who, me?" He lay still. He touched her breast gently with his forefinger; held it cupped. "Yes, yes indeed," he said.

"You idiot," she said. The hard edge had melted off her voice.

He felt soft and lazy, murmuring, "Yes, yes indeed."

Her hair had come undone; a twig and a few blades of grass were caught in the bright net of it. She loomed

21

above him, as eminent as if she leaned out of the sky. She seemed yielding and fiercely happy. Caught in the top limbs of the undergrowth behind her was a red round flicker he at first took to be a balloon. It bobbed, disappeared.

"Stop a minute," he said. He clasped the back of her hand, squeezed it firmly. "Wait . . . Let me up."

She got off and sat, clasping her knees with her forearms. He rose and the little fat man stepped out of the alder thicket. His face *was* like a balloon, red as catsup from wind and sun, and his grimy grin was so fixed it might have been painted. Yellowish whisker stubble was smeared on his chin and neck. He came forward in a sort of rolling slouch, his hands balled, stuffed into the pockets of his overalls. Under the overalls he wore no shirt and the fat on his chest moved with a greasy undulation as he breathed; one nipple was not covered by the bib of the overalls and it shone, obese; it was like the breast of a girl just come to puberty. Though he wore no shirt he wore a hat, a misshapen black felt object which looked as if it had been kicked a countless number of times. He must have been in his late fifties.

"Who are you?" Peter asked. Thin and ragged query.

"Well," he said. "I'm Ed Morgan. I live a little ways back over yonder." He jerked his thumb over his shoulder pointing north. "I was just kind of follerin' along the creek here. I've got me some mushrat traps strung out along the creek, and I was just checking up on them. Course it's a little late in the day, but I been busy all morning."

He didn't ask the question he wanted to, but the first one that came to his mind. "Why is it late in the day?"

The fat man gave him a wide ingenuous stare. "Why," he said, "a man ought to get down to his traps first thing in the morning. A mushrat'll just chew off his foot and get away. Or even if he is good and drownded might be an old mongrel dog'll come along and carry him off. I ought to got down here real early, but like I said I been busy this morning."

"Who gave you permission to trap along here?" In the fat man's manner there was a careless oily geniality, an attitude of unmovable self-possession, which irked Peter, made the muscles along his shoulder blades feel as if they might begin to twitch. He gave his question a flat tone.

"Well now, I guess nobody did," he said. "I never have thought about that. I just always have set out my traps here. My daddy did, and I reckon his daddy before him. Tell the truth, I was just getting ready to ask you folks what you was doing here. And then I thought maybe I better not." The dingy grin never left his face, not even when he jerked his head aside to loose a spate of tobacco.

Without moving his body he drew himself up stiffly. "I'm Peter Leland," he said. "I own this farm."

For what seemed a long time the old man just looked at him. "Well, I declare," he said finally. "You must be Miz Annie's grandbaby. I don't know how many times I've heard her tell all about you. She set a lot of store by you, you being a preacher and all. Law, she

23

was just as proud of you as a peacock. I don't believe there was ever what you'd call a whole lot of preachers in the Leland family."

He felt the fat man's eyes gauging him, measuring his weight, his probable worth. He would probably look at his caught muskrats in the same way. Peter felt nettled to the point of exasperation. "Am I to understand that you live on this farm?"

"Well, honey, I reckon so. Unless you was to take a notion to put me off. As far as I ever heard tell of, us Morgans has always lived right here on the Leland farm, and even before that, back when it was the old Jimson place. And no telling how long before that, no telling how long we might've been here."

His grin broadened slightly, and Peter had the impression that in the measuring of himself he had been found lacking. Not a pleasant impression. He let the muscles of his forearms relax and found, surprised, that since the little man had come he had been stifling the impulse to strike him in the face. This fat old man's assurance bordered upon, without trespassing into, cockiness. Peter sharply resented being called honey.

"No one told me there was a tenant family on the farm. Mr. Phelps didn't say a word about it." Mr. Phelps was the lawyer who had made the title arrangements, had done all the legal work.

Morgan lifted his hat, scratched the back of his head. Atop his head was a perfectly circular bald spot, the size and color of the crown of a large toadstool. "Well I declare I don't know," he said. "I guess maybe we been here so long now that folks just takes us for granted. All I know's we been here a long time." His gaze shifted momentarily. "Is that your pretty little wife?"

Sheila still sat on the grass, her knees caught to her chest. Again her face reddened slightly. She gave Morgan a short jerky nod.

"Yes, this is Mrs. Leland," Peter said. He was unwilling to say it; he felt somehow as if he were giving away an advantage.

"She sure is a pretty little thing," he said. "I reckon she's about the prettiest Leland woman I ever seen."

She pulled a weed, flung it down again, a gesture of overt annoyance.

He sharpened his tone, cut through the thread of this subject. "Where do you live then? I suppose you have a house on the farm." He felt that the brunt of her annoyance fell upon him rather than upon Morgan, and this exasperated him; it was unfair.

Again the old man jerked his thumb over his flaccid shoulder. "Just right up yonder, across the creek. You could see it from here if it wasn't for this here thicket. You want to come on over, I'll take you around. It ain't much, but it's what we're used to, what we've always had."

"I think maybe I'd better," Peter said. "I'd better see what I've got into." He turned to her. "Do you want to come along, sweetheart?"

She let drop another weed stem from her fingers. "Not this time," she said. She rose and brushed off her slacks with ostentatious care. "I'll go on back to the house. There's so much work I have to do."

"I'll be along shortly," he said, turning from her regretfully. Morgan had already started through the underbrush, parting the branches carelessly before him, letting them slap back.

Sheila began to gather the debris of the meal, piling everything into the basket. There was still a quarter bottle of wine. She screwed the cap more tightly, looking at the bottle with an almost sorrowful expression.

He followed along clumsily in Morgan's wake. The grass was strident with insects and an occasional saw brier clawed at his trousers legs. Once he almost tripped because the earth around the mouth of a muskrat hole crumbled under his foot. A very narrow footlog lay across the stream; the top of it was chipped flat, bore the marks of the hatchet, but worn smooth. Morgan crossed before him, his hands nonchalantly in his pockets, but Peter had to go gingerly, holding out his arms to balance himself. Once through the thicket on the other side of the creek, they could see Morgan's house. It was a low weather-stained cabin, nudged into the side of the hill so that while the east end of the house sat on the ground, the wall and the little porch on the west side were stilted up by six long crooked locust logs. There was a tin roof which didn't shine but seemed to waver, to metamorphose slightly, in the sunny heat. Few windows and dark, and a stringy wisp of smoke from the squat chimney. In a corner of the yard of hard-packed dirt below the house sat a darkened outhouse.

"There it is yonder," Morgan said. "I reckon you can tell it ain't much, but it's what we're used to. It'll do for us, I guess."

Before them lay what must once have been a fairly rich field of alfalfa; now it was spotted with big patches of Queen Anne's lace and ragweed, and the alfalfa looked yellow and sickly, its life eaten away at by the dodder parasite. Morgan waded through it cheerfully, obviously complacent about the condition of the crop, and Peter kept as much as possible in the fat man's footsteps. He felt that he didn't know what he might step into in that diseased field.

They went over the slack rusty barbed wire that enclosed the yard and went around the house to the low back stoop. There was a familiar kitchen clatter inside, but when Morgan stepped up on the wide slick boards all noise from inside ceased suddenly. He turned around, grinning still and even more broadly than before. "Come on in," he said. "We're just folks here."

He entered. At first he couldn't breathe. The air was hot and viscous; it seemed to cling to his hair and his skin. The black wood range was fired and three or four kettles and pans sat on it, steaming away industriously. The ceiling was low, spotted with grease, and all the heat lay like a blanket about his head. The floor was bare, laid with cracked boards, and through the spaces between them he could see the ground beneath the house. There was a small uncertain-looking table before the window on his right, and from the oilcloth which covered it large patches of the red-and-white pattern were rubbed away, showing a dull clay color. From the ceiling hung two streamers of brown flypaper which seemed to be perfectly useless; the snot-sized creatures crawled about everywhere; in an instant his hands and arms were covered with them. And through the steamy smell of whatever unimaginable sort of meal was cooking, the real odor of the house came: not sharp but heavy, a heated odor, oily, distinctly bearing in it something fishlike, sweetly bad-smelling; he had the quick impression of dark vegetation of immense luxuriance blooming up and momentarily rotting away; it was the smell of rank incredibly rich semen.

By the black range stood a woman who looked older than Morgan, her hair yellowish white, raddled here and there with gray streaks. She was huge, fatter even than Morgan, her breadth was at least half the length of the stove. She bulged impossibly in her old printed cotton dress and he shuddered inwardly at the thought of her finally bulging out of it, standing before him naked. In proportion to her great torso her arms and legs were very short and in tending her cooking she made slow short motions, she used her limbs no more than she had to, as if these were more or less irrelevant appendages. What was obviously important was the great fatness of her breasts, her belly, her thighs. She gave Peter a slow but only cursory look, turned her unmoved, unmoving gaze to Morgan. When Morgan introduced Peter she didn't acknowledge him by so much as a nod.

"This here's my wife Ina," Morgan said. "And this

here's my daughter Mina. She's the only one of our young'uns that's left with us now. The rest has all gone off different places, they couldn't find nothing to stay around here for, I guess. But Mina's stayed on with the old folks."

She sat at the weak-looking table. He couldn't guess her age, maybe fourteen or fifteen or sixteen. She sat playing with a couple of sticky strands of hair as black as onyx. She leaned back in a little creaky wooden chair and gave him a bald stark gaze. He felt enveloped in the stare, which was not a stare but simply an act of the eyes remaining still, those eyes which seemed as large as eggs, so gray they were almost white, reflecting, almost absolutely still. His skin had prickled at first, he had thought she had no nose, it was so small and flat, stretched on her face as smooth as wax. Leaned back in the chair that way, her body, flat and square, seemed as complacent as stone, all filled with calm waiting; this was her whole attitude. She played listlessly with her hair, looking at him. It was impossible. That body so stubby and that face so flatly ugly—something undeniably fishlike about it—and still, still it exercised upon him immediately an attraction, the fascination he might have in watching a snake uncoil itself lazily and curl along the ground. He couldn't believe it; maybe it was the crazy musky odor of the house, confusing all his impressions, his senses. He had to use his whole will to take his eyes off her.

"This here's Pete Leland," Morgan said. "He's the one that owns the place now, the whole farm. He's Miz

Annie's grandson, and he's a preacher. He's the only Leland I ever heard of that was a preacher."

Mina gave a soft slow nod, still looking at him, and it was directly to him that she spoke. "You're awful good-looking," she said. "You're so good-looking I could eat you up. I bet I could just eat you up." Her voice was soft and thick as cotton.

Morgan sniggered. "Don't pay her no mind," he said. "If you pay her any mind she'll drive you crazy, I swear she will."

But it had started and the whole while he walked back to the big brick house—going not the way he came, but following the winding red dirt road along the hillsides—her flat dark face hung like a warning lantern in his mind. He couldn't unthink her image.

THREE

Peter Leland would have admitted himself that his choice of the ministry as profession had risen hazy from his soiled smoky imagination. He would have admitted that he saw the Christian religion as a singularly uncheerful endeavor, and this he would have admitted as a fault in himself, one he felt powerless to remedy. It was simply that his black imagination forced him to take everything all too seriously, and exercised a partially debilitating influence on his work. He had, for instance, no very consoling bedside manner, and his hospital visits with members of his congregation turned out invariably to be extremely awkward affairs. And a few of his sermons might vie with some of Jonathan Edwards' for gloominess, though Peter lacked that zealous fire. One symptom of his racked fancy showed itself in his fantasies about his father, who had died when Peter was so young that he could not at all remember him. His father had died when the family lived here on the farm, and Peter's mother had

31

taken him away then to live with her and her parents in the eastern part of the state. Her family was pretty well off financially—her father owned an important electrical-appliance distributorship—and they were able to send Peter to the single large privately endowed university in the state. During his freshman year there his mother had died. Peter was shocked, grieved deeply, but he was not surprised. His mother had been long waning; she had always been a pale silent little woman, and this white quietude he had only half-consciously attributed to her grieving for his dead father. This was the one subject, at any rate, upon which she was completely reticent. The remarks of her family, that before her marriage she had been very gay and lively, he hardly credited; his observation wouldn't bear them out. When he had asked her how his father had died she had absolutely refused to speak of it, had only hinted that there was a terrifying disease of some sort. So that in his dark mid-adolescence he had begun to imagine that this disease was probably hereditary, had begun to wonder when it might overtake him also. He would imagine it as sudden and painlessly fatal, a black stifling area of wool dropped over him abruptly; or he would think of it as gradual and excruciating, a blob of soft metal dissolving in acid. And even when his adolescence was gratefully behind him he had never lost completely a secret vague conviction that his days were limited, that a deep bitter end awaited him at some random juncture of his life. This notion accounted in part for his mordant turn of mind, but still it was mainly a symptom: his whole nature was self-minatory.

And it was mostly because of this that he had become an active minister, for he would have enjoyed much more, and would have been more at ease in, a purely scholarly life. He would have much preferred the examination of Greek manuscripts and of his own looming conscience to the responsibility—he felt it a heavy responsibility—for the welfare of the souls of his little congregation of the First Methodist Church of Afton, North Carolina. His mind wouldn't let him rest in the leather-bound study. When he considered this inviting possibility a voice warning him that he was choosing a career of self-indulgence spoke in his head, and this voice he heeded without too regretful a delay. In his senior year and then during his years in the seminary he had armed himself the best he knew how to meet the world as an active, even a militant, Christian minister. That he had strange ideas about how to prepare himself to encounter the world was a consequence of his sheltered life. His mother had been understandably protective of him, and her family, curiously, had maintained her attitude. It was as if they shared some of his own premonition about his fate. They had been content somehow—they had seemed relieved—with his choice of profession and had willingly seen him through the seminary.

And despite the unworldliness of his younger life he had made a competent though hardly a thunderously successful minister. Perhaps it was the continued aware-ness of his own frailty which made him tolerant of the frailties of others, but his admonishment of the peccadilloes of his congregation—and in the town of Afton they were only peccadilloes—was couched in gentle terms gravely humorous. But the scholar in him *would* come out. A lecture concerning a historical problem of theology was sometimes offered them for a sermon; and they on their side were tolerant also. Perhaps they were pleased finally at having a preacher with brains, for their tolerance actually came to something more than that. Perhaps they even interpreted the intent of these scholarly discourses correctly, as gestures he wanted to make to indicate that even on the other side, out of the competitive fight which comprised the world they knew, it wasn't easy; that a faith doesn't drop as the gentle rain from heaven but is formed in continual intellectual and spiritual agony. Also it was simple enough to give a conventional sermonizing point to such discourse, for every genuine moral problem does ul-timately impinge on a man's daily life.

It was from one of his sermons, in fact, that his pres-ent project had emerged. Although the problem had at first been no more than a pretext for a sermon, when he had later pondered his own words the subject had seized him, and as much time as he could in conscience squeeze from his duties he devoted to a sketchy research. In time he decided to write a monograph, perhaps a book. He allowed himself a couple of months' vacation—the sudden inheriting of the farm was an almost unbelievable slice of luck—and from their inconsiderable savings account he had allowed himself three thousand dollars, even though he wasn't quite certain how all that money was to be utilized. "Three thousand is an outside figure," he told Sheila. For the sermon he had taken his texts from the First Book of Samuel, "And when they arose early on the morrow morning, behold, Dagon was fallen upon his face to the ground before the ark of the Lord; and the head of Dagon and both the palms of his hands were cut off upon the threshold; only the stump of Dagon was left to him. Therefore neither the priests of Dagon, nor any that come into Dagon's house, tread on the threshold of Dagon in Ashdod unto this day." Then he reminded them of Samson, delivered into the hands of the Philistines by the bitch Delilah. "Then the lords of the Philistines gathered them together for to offer a great sacrifice unto Dagon their god, and to rejoice: for they said, Our god hath delivered Samson our enemy into our hand." It was that temple of Dagon, he said, which Samson had destroyed with his hands, pulling it down with its pillars. Peter, seeming even taller in his perpendicular robe, pale and angular leaning forward in the pulpit, had informed his not very attentive audience that Dagon was simply one more of the pagan fertility deities; in Phoenicia his name was connected with the word *dagan*, meaning "corn," though this name finally derived from a Semitic root meaning "fish." He recalled the description by Milton in the catalogue of fallen angels:

35

Next came one
Who mourn'd in earnest, when the Captive Ark
Maim'd his brute Image, head and hands lopt off
In his own Temple, on the grunsel edge,
Where he fell flat, and sham'd his Worshipers:
Dagon his Name, Sea Monster, upward Man
And downward Fish.

He had noted how the figure of Dagon had attached to the sensibilities of Renaissance historians, his story being told by Selden, Sandys, Purchas, Ross, and by Sir Walter Raleigh in his history of the world. The congregation shifted from ham to ham, resentfully itchy under this barrage of verse and unfamiliar names. But Peter had continued to read from his notes, saying that the human imagination had been hard put to it to let go this crippled fertility figure. The worship of Dagon had even traveled to America. He read to them from William Bradford's history of the Plymouth colony the story of Mount Wollaston:

After this they fell to great licentiousness and led a dissolute life, pouring out themselves into all profaneness. And Morton became Lord of Misrule, and maintained (as it were) a School of Atheism. And after they had got some goods into their hands, and got much by trading with the Indians, they spent it as vainly in quaffing and drinking, both wine and strong waters in great excess. . . . They also set up a maypole, drinking and dancing about it many days together, inviting the Indian women for their consorts, dancing and frisk-

ing together like so many fairies, or furies, rather; and worse practices. As if they had anew revived and celebrated the feasts of the Roman goddess Flora, or the beastly practices of the mad Bacchanalians. Morton likewise, to show his poetry composed sundry rhymes and verses, some tending to lasciviousness, and others to the detraction and scandal of some persons, which he affixed to this idle or idol maypole. They changed also the name of their place, and instead of calling it Mount Wollaston they call it Merry-mount, as if this jollity would have lasted ever. But this continued not long, for after Morton was sent for England . . . shortly after came over that worthy gentleman Mr. John Endecott, who brought over a patent under the broad seal for the government of Massachusetts. Who, visiting those parts, caused that maypole to be cut down and rebuked them for their profaneness and admonished them to look there should be better walking. So they or others now changed the name of their place again and called it Mount Dagon.

Here he had closed his notes and in the few minutes remaining he preached in earnest. The worship of Dagon, he said, still persisted in America. The characteristics which had made this god attractive to men were clearly evident in the society that encircled them. Didn't the Dagon notion of fertility dominate? Frenzied, incessant, unreasoning sexual activity was invited on all sides; every entertainment, even the serious entertainments, the arts, seemed to suppose this activity as basis.

This blind sexual Bacchanalia was inevitably linked to money—one had only to think of the omnipresent advertisements, with all those girls who alarmed the eye. A mere single example. And wasn't the power of money finally dependent upon the continued proliferation of product after product, dead objects produced without any thought given to their uses? Weren't these mostly objects without any truly justifiable need? Didn't the whole of American commercial culture exhibit this endless irrational productivity, clear analogue to sexual orgy? And yet productivity without regard to eventual need was, Peter maintained, actually unproductivity, it was really a kind of impotence. This was the paradox which the figure of Dagon contained. To worship Dagon was to worship a maimed, a mutilated god, a god to whom "only the stump" remained. Dagon had lost both head and hands, only his loins remained; and below the waist he was fish, most unthinking of animals. Dagon was symbol both of fertility and infertility; he represented the fault in mankind to act without reflecting, to *do* without knowing why, to go, without knowing where. Was it simply coincidence that Merrymount had changed its name to Mount Dagon after Endicott had chopped down the maypole? Or might it not be a continuation of the worship of crippled sexuality? The ruined Dagon and the chopped maypole mirrored each other too clearly, didn't they? It couldn't be coincidence. But even if these manifestations were independent they still emerged from that human sickness, the worship of uncaring physical discharge, onanism, impotence, nihilism hurtling at a superspeed. It was this unconscious regard that he wished them to root from their hearts. He insisted that a Christian life was of necessity a reflective life, that useless movement, unresting expenditure of substance and spirit, was alien to it. He exhorted them to continual vigilance. He admitted that it wasn't an easy thing he asked.

Here he ended, and was aware for the first time of the weighty boredom his words had created.

His congregation sat before him listless as sun-bleached stones. He looked at them tiredly, then looked at Sheila sitting before him in her encouraging front pew. Her yellow hair shone bright, falling over the shoulders of her dark blue dress. She grinned. Her torso rose and fell with the burden of a heavy mock sigh. With the back of her hand she wiped away imaginary sweat from her forehead. . . . Anger flooded him momentarily. If it was a dull sermon for her, tough luck. It had been for him an earnest try, he had said something that he honestly cared about. His wife, for God's sake, ought to stand with him. . . . But the effort was too much after the long sermon and his anger evaporated. He was merely annoyed and tired. He answered her with a resigned shrug and announced the final hymn. "Let us sing number 124, 'Thou hidden love of God,'" he said. "Let us please sing only the first and last verses." He reckoned on a long afternoon of relentless teasing—half-serious—from his bright pretty wife.

And in some ways he dreaded it. As an intellectual

opponent she was formidable, and once she had caught him in an awkward position she wouldn't let up. This was an attitude of hers he couldn't help resenting at times, even though he recognized that it was an attitude which his own nature needed for any kind of wholesome balance. If he had been deliberately shopping for temperaments, he couldn't have got better than Sheila's— wry, tough, at times baldly sarcastic—as an antidote for his own pessimistic nature, which was too often unwillingly pompous. Marriage with a gloomier, less sceptical nature would surely have been consummated in a suicide pact. Sheila simply refused to take him as seriously as he took himself. "All that nonsense . . ." He couldn't help, in a way, envying her her full generosity of movement and feeling; but he was simply not like that, he was too knotted, ponderous. She would twit him then, he took it as one takes a too-acid medicine: *it tastes so bitter, it must do some good.* He would like to have the barrier broken, that wall between him and the ordinariness of life. This he genuinely wanted, to prank and disport in the tepid waters of dailiness, of pettiness, of the trivia which comprise existences. He would like to spend hours dawdling over his morning coffee, or choosing which socks to buy or which greeting card to send. But he was as he was, not even Sheila could break that down. An enervating sense of guilt drove him to study, to learn, to preach, to visit, to harass, to perform good works. He could not answer the question whether works properly good could proceed from an exaggerated feeling of guilt; neither could he suppress the question.

But there was Sheila. She had married him as soon as he was out of seminary, though their contact in those four years had been through letters almost entirely. The courtship and actual wooing had gone on before, when he was at the university where she was a student. She had lasted out the four-year wait easily enough, rather gaily; and he couldn't help wondering if her nature didn't demand his as much as his demanded hers. His faults were the faults of solidity, and perhaps the solidity was what she needed to attach to. It might be all too easy for her free humor to fog away into frivolity. A comforting thought, her need for him; made him feel less parasitic. . . . She was a fine girl, would be a fine mother, but though they had been married four years— he was now thirty-two—there were no children. The childlessness bothered Peter; he felt it almost as a debt he owed and which he might be called upon to pay at any time, any moment when he would be unprepared. Simply one more instance of the way his impending fate would catch him up helpless.

"Why didn't you just read us the whole encyclopedia?" she asked. She dished out pertly the cool Sunday luncheon salad. "That really would have been entertaining."

"I'm not so sure you ought to come to church to be entertained," he said.

"Wow. You can say that again."

"Maybe you should come with a reasonable hope for edification."

She peeped at him tartly. "Do you know what hell is? It's edification without entertainment. Big mountains of boredom."

His anger wouldn't come back, he felt empty. "Oh, come on. It wasn't that bad, was it?"

"I don't know. How bad did you want it to be?"

"I didn't want it to be bad at all. Matter of fact, I thought it was pretty interesting myself. Sort of sexy."

"That's because it's an idea you found. That's the reason you like it. I doubt if any of it applies much to people now. It all seemed so . . . historical. So distant."

"But that's the point. I don't think it is. Didn't you listen to the last part? I was trying to show the pertinence . . ."

"Yes, yes. I heard. But I don't like it."

She got up abruptly and left the table. He felt morose and dissatisfied. But she came back in a few minutes and poured the coffee.

"Hurry up and drink that down. I want to find out firsthand all this crazy wild endless American sex you keep talking about."

FOUR

The work wasn't coming along so easily. The idea still
held him, it still seemed a valid and terrifying notion,
but so far he hadn't unpacked his notes and books and
papers. He would sleep late in the mornings, a habit
alien to him, would lie tossing in the tall dark bed in
the upstairs bedroom they had chosen. Dreams tortured
him, jerking him awake sweating and with a dusty
acrid taste in his mouth, but he was unable to remember
these dreams; he could recall only dark queer impressions, odors. Then when he rose and had eaten—for
some reason his appetite had increased; he who had
never really cared for food seemed now always hungry
—he wandered about the house, not speaking much; and
in the afternoons he would take long walks over the
farm, usually alone. Now and then, with nothing he
could perceive to trigger it, the queer face of Mina
would pop into his mind, and always at her image his
stomach felt queasy, his skin prickly. He complained
a great deal.

"Sure enough," Sheila said, "I've never seen you so restless."

"I just can't get started."

"I wouldn't worry about it so much. I've always heard that people who write things have to go a long time sometimes when they can't write. Professional writers and people, I mean."

"This isn't like that." He wished that he didn't sound so abrupt.

She shrugged. "I wouldn't worry about it too much. You deserve a nice vacation, anyway."

"Not till I've really done something."

The house managed to occupy much of his attention. It was large enough to explore: sixteen rooms in all, not counting the many closets and areaways and the tall attic. Standing in a room on another floor and at the opposite end of the building he could sense Sheila's movements; that was how alive the house was for him. The pleasure he took in poking about was rather a morose pleasure—like so many of his pleasures. He opened trunks and drawers and stood contemplating the masses of stiff gauzy dresses and dark woolen shirts and trousers. Uncomfortable as the clothing looked he had sometimes to suppress the impulse to dress himself in it, to try to find out, like a child, exactly how his grandparents had felt in it. Now it seemed to him, as he became more closely acquainted with the house, that all his surmises about his grandparents had been only partially correct, that he had missed something central, something essential about them that he could discover in

44

himself if only he looked hard enough. It was not all just soured Puritanism, it was something even darker, if that were possible. One trunk was almost filled with correspondence and received Christmas cards and beneath these, lying loose, about three dozen shotgun shells of varying gauges; but there was no gun in the house. In one drawer was a small tin box half filled with dynamite caps. The correspondence was impossible. Very few of the letters were signed and the writing was always illegible, always bordering upon illiteracy. "Our if i ca'nt pay that much Why then i will exspect just what You had oferd the 1st time . . . my legel rites ech time . . . the religiun you clame to profess." There were words so entirely illegible they looked almost like transliterations from some exotic tongue, ancient Pnakotic perhaps: "Nephreu," "Yogg Sothoth," "Ka nai Hadoth," "Cthulhu." The effort he spent in trying to decipher these letters tired him, and he sometimes got headaches staring at the dimmed writing in bad light. He felt that the letters were obscurely responsible for the bad dreams that came on him late in the mornings. The letters coated his hands with a dust that he had almost to scrape off.

Sheila regarded his explorations with her usual amused tolerance, but this attitude of hers which he had always so needed now rankled him. He felt childish enough on his own without her rubbing it in. She found things enough to do. She kept herself busy with the house; keeping clean just the four or five rooms that they used was almost a day-long task. And she was making a dress, using the old foot-treadle sewing machine which sat in a downstairs hall. The awkward intermittent clacking of it sang through the house with a sound like a hive of bees. When Peter passed by her as she worked, just wandering through, she looked up and grinned at him in what she had to begin to hope was a friendly manner, but he didn't grin back. He laid a tactless absent-minded hand on her shoulder and wandered away, just passing by.

The attic was the worst. It was narrow but tall, and admitted light through a single small round window, like a porthole, high, just under the arch of the roof. But the light that entered, acrid yellow light, filled the whole space. The light locked with the dust— tons of dust up here—and the atmosphere of the place stuffed his head like a fever. The yellow light was blinding and hot; he breathed slowly and deliberately. It seemed that he perceived this light with every nerve in his body. The attic was mostly empty. On the left side the naked rafters ran down, and here and there nails had been driven into them to hold up a couple of wool coats, which looked almost steamy in the heat, and a couple of long plaited tobacco bed canvases. Piled on the floor were thick sheaves of newspapers, brittle and yellow like the light, and in the light the printed words were withering into unintelligibility. When he nudged a thick folded paper with his toe, it slid forward silently in the thick dust.

In his head the sight of Mina's face bobbed backward and forward like an empty floating bottle.

Against the right wall—which was simply ranked joists and nude lathes through which hardened plaster seemed to be oozing—sat a broken sausage grinder and a small empty keg over the mouth of which generations of spiders had stretched webs. Toward the south, the wall where the light entered, there was a queer arrangement of chains. At the angle where the attic floor and two joists met, two thick spikes were driven through two chain links, pinching each chain tightly into the wood. The chains, large chains, ran up each joist to a height of about eight feet, secured at intervals by big hasps, and then from this height they dangled down about a foot. Attached to the ends of the chains were broad iron bands which looked something like colters for plow tongues except that they were hinged on one side so that they could open and shut. Snap. The lock for each chain was some sort of internal affair—the bands were at least a half-inch thick. There was a fairly flexible tongue, notched on one side only, which slipped into the band itself, and on the top of the band was a tiny lever which could be wiggled back and forth. Obviously this lever released the ratchet inside the band so that it could be opened. The chains looked red in the yellow light; he had spent a long time looking at them. He held one of the bands with his index finger and swung it gently. A soft unnerving creak as the chain rubbed against the top hasp. He estimated that the empty oval the band enclosed was about four inches in diameter the long way. He stroked his finger along the inside of the band and it came away reddish. Rust, he

47

thought; but it didn't flake, it wasn't gritty like rust. He stood on tiptoe and examined the opening where the band was hinged, where it would pinch. Small hairs gleamed yellow on the red iron, hairs like the down on arms, or eyelashes. His eyes were wide. He sucked his lips. He put the band about his wrist and snapped it shut. It fit exactly; he nodded. And if his other wrist was in the other cuff he wouldn't be able to reach the little lever to free himself. Standing flat he had a sensation of lightness, of dizzy buoyancy, his arm dangling upward like that. The iron was at first cool, then warm; his wrist began to sweat a little in it. Immediately he felt thirsty.

I could just eat you all up, she had said. *I could just throw you down and jerk all your clothes off,* she said.

He swung his arm idly; it wasn't so uncomfortable after all. Iron rasped on iron. He turned his wrist round in the cuff and, yes, it did pinch and pull at the hinge opening. He thumbed the release lever and it went over quite easily, too easily, and the cuff didn't open. He flipped the lever back and forth and jerked his wrist hard again and again. Then he stood quite still. Plumes of dust rose and settled reluctantly, the yellow motes spiraling down. It was clear that he wasn't going to get himself loose. He tried to remember where in the house he had run across the large old file. Could he signal Sheila? She was on the first floor, busy at something. He shouted twice, and his voice seemed muffled even to himself. The sound locked with the dust and lay silent on the floor. His feet were shuffling, and he

48

sneezed twice, three times. Up here it was simply life-
less; the house which was so alive everywhere else was
dead at the top. Or perhaps Sheila was insensitive to the
liveliness of the house. He reached to the other cuff and
grasped the margin of chain above it and swung the
cuff against the joist. He banged it again and again and
he could see that the joist was throbbing quite soundly,
he could feel the floor reverberating beneath his feet,
but when he stopped banging he heard no footsteps. She
wasn't coming; she hadn't heard. And then he did hear
footsteps, but they didn't come closer, didn't go anywhere at all. It was just his imagination; no one was
walking.

She had no nose, Mina, any more than a fish. She
deeped in oceans of semen.

The dust rose to his waist, not so violently yellow now.
Time was passing, the light was growing less virulent.
He leaned against the wall, trying not to breathe too
deeply, but it was no good; he kept sneezing and sneezing, and his eyes filled with water, which made the light
go all bright again. How could she not feel the house
quiver when he hammered? It shuddered all over, the
whole fabric of it was shaken. He banged with the
chain for a while and then stopped again. His legs
ached, it was unbearable. The guts had rusted in the cuff
lock, he must have known. Not rust but blood his finger
had searched out on the iron cuff; it was old caked
blood, it didn't flake like rust. It had got later and
later. His mind and his eyes had got full of fear and the
house was full of sounds, all the wrong kind, scraping

49

and slithering. It was as though iron were freezing on his legs. He was trying to take shallow breaths, for when he breathed deeply he had to choke and sneeze; but thinking about it made it impossible and he would finally have to take a long deep breath, and the coughing would turn into retching.

The thought came to him, as immediate as the binding iron, that this was where his father had died. There wasn't evidence, his mind didn't need evidence, the whole house was full of the fact. His mind was full of the house. The cuff fitted exactly. The image in his head was an event he had already experienced; had stood here with both arms chained, fallen against the hot wall and sweating furiously in the clothes he had fouled all over. He didn't think he could manage to live through it again. But then he realized that the man he knew, both arms locked in the chains, was too short and he carried too much flesh. . . . They had told him his father had died when he was four. He was a shorter man than his son, the chains wouldn't reach down so far for him; his arms he must have wrenched from their sockets almost. And why had they brought him, Peter, up here to see? His father, not mad, but furiously raging in inhuman anger, with the sweat all over him like yellow paint. His shattered eyes. What was it they had wanted him to see?

He could not see. There was only a round whitish glow in the top of the wall, noseless, unreadable as Mina. In the darkness objects, the broken sausage mill, the hanging coats, had seeped over their edges, occupied space where they had no mass. Now it was night; the house multiplied its imagined noises which would advance and advance certainly and never arrive. But under the narrow door a soft thick pane of light appeared, arced and disappeared; appeared again.

He heard her. "Peter? Peter? Are you up here?"

"Here," he said. He didn't say it. His throat was clogged. He croaked, his mouth was thick and helpless.

When she opened the door the draught blew up the dust, invisible now in the darkness. And he coughed and then gagged; wiped his caked mouth on his hanging arm. He imagined how he would look to her, he would frighten her to death; he turned his head to face the light and made his black lips smile. She was holding a kerosene lamp she had found somewhere in the house. He tried to hold his breath again, but drew it in hard and shuddering. It was Mina, it was not Sheila. He was almost weeping and he turned his face away, then turned to look again. . . . No. It was Sheila, with the darkness gathered on her blond hair, and with the lamp held before her and low like that so that her nose had no outlines, looked gone.

"A fuse must have blown, I think," she said. "This is all the light I could find. What are you doing up here, anyway?" She held the light close; she could just make him out as yet.

He got the smile back, tried to fix it.

"My God." She saw him.

He kept hoping she wouldn't drop the lamp. The attic would burn, go up like a box of matches.

51

"My God, Peter . . ."

His speech was like bitter black syrup. "There's a big file in the top drawer of the chest in the downstairs hall, if you could . . ."

She came to him. The warmth of the lamp spread on his face and neck. "What is . . ."

"If you could get the file. Sheila." He couldn't be franker in begging.

She stared at his face and then stared away, looking into the glow of the lamp. She had turned the wick too high; sooty threads of smoke rose from the lamp and the bulbous chimney was still blackening. "Yes," she said. When she turned from him her shadow was huge, fell like thick musty cloth on the whole room, on him. Gathered around the light her shape was bunched and dark and it was licked up softly by the dust and fear of the room. He felt relieved when she went out the door, but then she would have to come back again. He feared for her. It was as bad, the way she found him, as he had imagined. He felt a terrifying pity for her.

His legs felt as if they would topple any moment; trembled, trembled. He heard her going down the stairs, and then after that a complete unexpected silence. There were no noises now to imagine. He hawked up sticky spittle, rolled his tongue in it, licked his lips. They tasted acrid, felt puffy.

When she came back she seemed to have regained herself. She came quickly and confidently toward him, holding the file in her left hand. "I declare," she said, "just like a child. I don't see how you could get yourself

52

into such a predicament. Just like a child, can't stay out of trouble."

He took the file she held out. "I need water," he said. "I don't think I can do it without water." He began rubbing immediately at the bottom of a chain link.

"I declare," she said. She went away again.

In the darkness he rubbed hastily at the chain and then his arm would tire and he would have to stop. He had begun sweating again, and as he worked he was panting. He thought about how silly he must look and he felt very clearly that someone was watching him, noted amusedly his every motion, even his thoughts: Mina.

She came back with the water. "I brought a whole bunch of water," she said. "You seemed to want it pretty badly." She set down a galvanized pail half-filled. Inside, a metal cup rolled about slowly. "Here," she said, giving him the cup.

The first gulps turned the thickness in his mouth into a slick coagulant film and he spat the water out. It dropped in the dust with a sound like rope dropping. He began to swallow hard; he wanted it so much he felt he could almost bite it. He squatted dizzily and dipped his hand into the water and smeared it on his face. Immediately the dust was in it, his face darkening. He went back to his filing.

Sheila was all right, better than he had expected. "Do you know how they catch monkeys for zoos, monkeys out in the jungle? They make a hole in the coconut shell—they have the shell tied tight first, of course—and inside they put some kind of small nuts a monkey

53

likes. The hole is just large enough for him to get his hand in, but when he clenches his hand to hold the nuts, then the hole is too small and he can't get loose. He's too stingy or too stupid to let go the nuts. That's how they do it. But you know, I never really believed that they could capture monkeys that way until I saw you standing here with your hand caught like that. And not even having the excuse of nuts or whatever to get you to stick your hand in. Did you ever stick your hand in the fire because it looked so nice and hot? I don't mean now, I know you're too smart to do something like that now; but when you were younger, maybe. Maybe when you were in college?"

He shook his head, keeping the grimness of his face away from her. He had got the link through in one place now and had begun to make a new cut. He thought that she was talking in order to quell her nervousness. He sweated heavily, wishing that he hadn't dirtied the water in the pail; the thirst was on him again.

"But you know, when I couldn't find you, I honestly just knew it was something like this, I honestly did. The way you've been poking about into every nook and cranny in this house a person would think you were expecting to find a fortune, a pot of gold. Behind a secret panel or something like that. Really. I've never seen anyone so dopey about something before. Of course, that's your way—I know it—if there's anything at all around you can take as seriously as cancer, you'll do it. Know what? Watching you wander around all mopey like that, I've just wanted to tell you that if the house bothered you all that much we could get a tent and set up in the fields. Or if you were really bothered we could go home. But you wouldn't let loose of the house, not for anything. Just like those monkeys they catch."

He was almost free now, but he had to stop. The muscles in his forearm were jerking from the fiery exertion. She went on talking and now he wished she would be quiet, just hush up. He stroked his forearm against his thigh and wiped the sweat from his face on his left shoulder where his shirt was already wet and filthy from the reflex. He went back to work.

". . . And if you think I'm giving you a hard time, you're right," she said. "And don't think you don't deserve it, every bit."

The longer length of chain slapped against the wall, rebounded. His arm plummeted, the cuff banged against his thigh; there would be a bruise there. He was free. He sat down, hugging his knees, pain rushing to them. He put his head on his knees. His seeing was contracting and expanding in circles. He was almost weeping.

At last he stood up, Sheila helping him. "Let's go down," he said. He took the lamp from her, turned down the wick, and they went down together. He had retained the file; the four links dangled from the cuff, touched his leg. Stranger than ever, the house in the moving lamplight; shadows deeper and alive, shifting upon themselves. The varnished furniture reflected the dull glow in spots like dull eyes. They were enclosed in the lamp's burning, he leaning slightly against her, dirty, tired, musing, the chain flopping; she took his weight on her shoulder, her arm thrown over his shoulders, her hand gripping his shirt.

In the kitchen they let go. He set the lamp on the drainboard of the sink, ran cold water on his face and hair, shaking his head. When he straightened the water streaked his shirt. "Okay," he said. "I'll take a look at the fuse box." Now she took the lamp and followed him to the short hallway by the kitchen. He didn't open the box. "The switch is thrown," he said. His foot encountered something soft and warm, and he bent and picked up a heavy woolen overcoat; blue this one was. The house was cluttered with them. "This coat," he said, "it must have got hung on the switch here. The weight of it pulled the power off."

She put her fingers on her open mouth, all embarrassed. "I was just straightening up," she said. "I didn't know that it . . . I'm sorry." She brushed her chin lightly, a gesture of disbelief. "I'm sorry."

He threw the switch. All the lights went on. Everything looked naked now, the walls, the furniture; and they seemed naked too and turned away from each other as if in shame. Only for a moment. He took the lamp from her and screwed the wick down almost out of sight; a fragile bloom of black smoke rose from the chimney where the flame went out. "Here." He handed her the heavy coat and she took it, not quite meeting his gaze yet, and hugged it to her. The tail of it fell, hiding her body. She stared at him. "I really am sorry," she said. "Really."

He tapped the cuff on his wrist with the big file.

56

"I'm going to get this off," he said, "and then I'm going to take a bath. Hot water and six bars of soap."

"All right," she said. "Good enough. And I'll fix us some supper. It must be nine o'clock."

He considered. "None for me, though. I really don't feel like eating."

"Well . . . How about coffee then?"

"Coffee, fine."

FIVE

He had found a little straight chair with a sagging cane bottom and he sat there in the short hallway slowly and steadily rasping at the cuff. The grainy powder dripped on his shoes. He figured he could cut through on one edge where the cuff snapped shut and then cut through the tongue. Then he would be free. There was no hurry now, but fear wouldn't leave him. He had seen his father like that, a short man with huge terrifying eyes. Inheriting the farm he had inherited Mina, inheriting the house he had inherited chains. There was more to come, something was catching up with him. He had never considered that fright could have such dimensions as when Sheila had brought in the lamp, he taking her for Mina. He ought to see the girl again; of course, she was only poor and ordinary. It was the house and the isolation working in his head. Incongruous images falling together all silly. But he could not convince himself; all his thoughts, and even his body, lacked conviction.

How well, really, was he remembering?

He has lost the way, his grandmother said. But her voice couldn't have sounded the way it did in his mind, like metal creaking on metal; no one had ever sounded like that—it was the way her image in the tinted photograph in the sun parlor would speak. *He has lost the way, now see what he has come to. You will too if you ever get lost like your father.* He was squirming to get away from her, struggling not to see, but her fingers, complacently strong as iron, held his wrists. He would not look at the attic wall, but he could not help looking. Now he felt that he had been called upon to judge his father, but now he did not know the standards by which judgment was to be made. He stopped the filing and rubbed his nose. Perhaps in his first encounter with the house he had been correct: those standards had disappeared from the earth forever. . . . No. . . .

What was certain was that he couldn't quench the image of Mina; it came to his mind ever more insistently. The confusion between Mina and his wife seemed incredible, even with the crouched darkness and the bad light. It could be explained only by expectancy; he had been convinced that it was Mina who would come through that door. And her face remembered was intractable entirely; it wouldn't respond to any maneuver of his imagination, it offered no similes, as totally itself as the taste of garlic. But what did it mean? Why did it drift in his thought unattached, coming and going like a light winking an indecipherable code?

The cuff dropped to the cool tile floor and he let the file drop too, his right hand hot from the pressure of it.

59

The weight of the iron he still felt on his wrist. He leaned forward to rest, his elbows on his knees. Then he straightened in his chair and kicked the gaping iron ring as hard as he could. It slid across the floor, struck the wall and rebounded, came slithering back and touched against his foot. He rose and went down the hall to the bathroom, rubbing his wrist.

He leaned over the ugly yellowing tub which sat high on four legs with claw feet, and pushed in the plug. He breathed gratefully the steam that rose when he drew the hot water; he had been afraid that the power had been off so long the water would be cold in the tank. When he saw his face in the little streaked cabinet mirror he wasn't shocked, but regretfully assured instead. His eyes and mouth seemed holes poked in stiff gray paper. His eyes were pink-edged, his hair stiff and spiky with the clotted dust. While the water was drawing he washed his face at the little chipped lavatory. The water made his wrist itch and burn and he saw there the broad raw ichorous streak the iron had put on him. Then he stripped; his shirt and undershirt came off reluctantly, plastered to his skin with sweat and grime. He held them at arm's length, they were almost unrecognizable. He let them drop, he had decided to burn them. He climbed into the tub and lolled back, just letting the water lap into the dust. After a while he began to scrub earnestly and the water became almost inky. He had to let it out and draw a new tub.

He lay there, eyes closed, resting in the new water. He heard the door open and looked to see Sheila enter-

ing, her full arms cradled. He watched her face, pink
and oval but with the sharp chin, a face like a brightly
buffed fingernail. "Well," she said, "you seem well out
of danger now."

"I think I'll live." He spoke very slowly, his throat
still feeling dense. "I hope to God."

"I brought you some clean clothes and things. You
think maybe that will help?"

"It'll be fine. How about the coffee?"

"You want it now—in the bathtub?" Then, seeing
his expression: "Oh. Okay. I'll go get it. It ought to be
about ready now."

In a while she came back, carrying cup and saucer,
balancing them with exaggerated care in her left hand.
He sat up and reached for it, but she stepped back
sharply. The coffee slopped into the saucer. "My God,"
she said. "Look at your wrist. It looks horrible. Just
look at your poor wrist."

He was totally ashamed; dropped his injured hand
into the water, hid it behind his naked left thigh. "It's
nothing," he said.

"It's *not* nothing. It's all torn up. Here, let me see it.
We're going to have to do something about that. It looks
just awful."

"It's all right, it's nothing."

She searched his face with the cool gray gaze. It felt
like a spray of cold water on him. He discovered that
he wanted to cower away from her stare; now she had
the goods on him, now she knew his whole guilt. She
stepped carefully away from him and around and set

61

the cup and saucer atop the cistern of the toilet. Then she came back, sat on the tub edge. "It's not all right. How can you say that? It's raw and bleeding. . . . Here." She reached for the wrist, but he jerked it away, behind his back.

"No," he said.

She straightened herself, shook water from her gleaming plump hand. She began to talk slowly, in a quiet voice. "Peter, what is it? What's been wrong with you lately? What happened up there in that attic?"

He shook his head. "Nothing; nothing happened. I was just being silly, messing around with those chains."

"That's not right." She too shook her head, setting the blond strands atwitch. "I've never seen you like that. I've never seen anyone like that." She rubbed her eyes with her forearm. "I hope I never see anybody in such a state again."

She was merciless. He waited, but finally had to speak. "There's nothing wrong. I just got too curious about the chains. Like the monkeys you were talking about. There's not much that can happen to a fellow alone in an attic, after all." And now he felt that he was betraying her, betraying both of them. But, really, wasn't it merely a harmless lie designed to shelter her feelings?

"Oh, that's not right, that's not right at all." Verge of exasperation. "You know it's not like that. . . . Because it's been going on too long. There's been something wrong with you ever since we got to the farm."

"What's that? What are you talking about?" A question meant to embarrass her, to force her to describe behavior for which there was no good description; thus, to draw from her an accusation because of the lack of concreteness. Perhaps an accusation was what he most wanted. . . .

She skirted the trap as easily as a plump dowager, lifting her hem demurely, would avoid a puddle. She looked at his dampening forehead. "I don't think this place is healthy for you, I know it's not. I don't think we ever should have come here."

Now he knew he was on safer ground, but he didn't feel any more confident. "That's pretty silly, don't you think? I mean, really; it sounds like something out of a horror story or a Bela Lugosi movie or something. . . . It doesn't really mean anything, does it?"

She rose slowly (but she was angry) and began walking up and down, taking precise military strides like a man. How often it had seemed to Peter that she was a man, maybe more male in the way it counted than he. . . . "Don't you do that," she said. Baldly warning tone. "Don't you patronize me. Don't say to me, *I mean, really*. You're not the kind to patronize, you don't have the weight. And you know me too well. You know I don't talk just to be talking."

"I didn't mean it that way. Of course I didn't. But you'll have to admit, the way you put it, it does seem sort of silly and made-up."

"No, it doesn't." She was behind him now, standing still. Her voice was tight and even. "But you've made up your mind not to talk to me about it. You don't even know whether you ever will talk to me again. You're as transparent as a child. Fuck you, just fuck you, Peter Leland."

He turned amazed, his torso jerked round, and she flung at him the cup of coffee. Her face was hot and white, pale as her eyes. She threw it at him with the awkward grace of a ten-year-old boy. —The fierce coffee splashed on his shoulder and side. The cup smashed on one of the tub faucets. Coffee, the dark stain, spread in the water like a storm filling the sky. He could not speak, could not think; could never have guessed her violence. She did not relent. She marched out, again tightly military, not glancing at him. Going away, she held her back and shoulders stiff. She didn't slam the door, didn't close it. The cold air of the hall poured in on him.

He could not speak, he could not smile at her rage. He had never felt less humorous. He got up very slowly and carefully. It was hard to see the chips of the broken cup in the darkened water. He sat poised on the edge of the tub, searching the floor. There lay the slim curved handle of the cup, retaining its identity in a surprising manner. He picked his way tiptoe over the floor and put on his underwear and his socks and shoes. Then he felt safer, but no better. He picked up the shards from the floor and dropped them into the toilet; he drained the tub, but let the broken china remain.

Then he felt that he had nothing to do, he was at a loss. Had it really been so bad, trapped in the chains? He went through, sensing the whole presence of the house about him, and in the kitchen took down cup and saucer and poured coffee. A package of Sheila's menthol-flavored cigarettes lay on the table and he got one out and lit it, though he was not a smoker. He hadn't tried to smoke since he was sixteen years old. The sensation was surprising; it tasted slightly medicinal, but not at all unpleasant. He puffed assiduously and felt gratified. He drank the coffee slowly. Then he rose; he felt, rather than heard, Sheila's movements in the upstairs bedroom. She was readying for bed.

He went back through the house again, turning out the lights, and he mounted the stairs in the dark, sliding his hand along the solid cool banister. As he went up, it came to him how the things in the house, the furniture, even the stairs and the walls, seemed important to him, seemed to mean intelligible puzzling comments, while things not connected with the house, with his new knowledge—whatever sort it was—did not touch and were unimportant. Even alien, perhaps. What real connection did Sheila have with the house, with his past? With *him?* The thought felt true, that she was an intruder, nettlesome.

She lay in the bed with her face turned away from him toward the wall. The bed had a high solid headboard, about six feet tall, and was dark, like almost all the furniture in the house. Her pale head looked small, settled at the bottom of the headboard, not larger than a thumbnail. It would be best not to speak to her. She had left only the lamp on the big dark vanity burning, and by this light he undressed. His body was reflected in the three mirrors. He looked extremely pallid —the lamp was very small and had a clear white shade —but he looked dark too somehow. It was as if his body gathered some of the darkness of the furnishings, or as if it had been tinged by the thick obscurity of the attic. Especially about his eyes the shadows stayed, and the eyes too looked dark and liquescent, reflecting only in pinpoints the light of the lamp. He was extremely thin and ribby, as if there were just barely enough skin to cover him. But it all seemed natural.

He turned off the lamp, went cautiously through the dark to the bed and clambered awkwardly in. The sheets were of coarse cotton, but they felt soothing. He stretched his thin legs and then let them relax, and it seemed he could feel strength draining into them again. He hadn't quite realized how exhausted he had become. He spoke softly, "Sheila." But she wouldn't answer; her body didn't respond to his voice even by a movement of aversion. It was no good trying to talk to her now. Wearily he began to wonder exactly what there was between them that he had to patch up; he honestly couldn't say what the quarrel was about. And he abruptly put it out of his mind, just shrugged it away, and fell asleep.

A bitter sleep, immediately shot through with yellow sick dreaming. He was still himself, but somehow impersonally so, huge, monolithic. There was no one else, but there were momentary impressions of great deserted cities which flashed through his consciousness, gleaming white cities with geometries so queer and dizzying as to cause nausea. And when the cities remained stationary they were immediately engulfed by a milky-white odorous ocean. This same smelly chalky sea water was attacking him also and he began to dissolve away; he was becoming transparent, he was a mere threadlike wraith, merely a long nerve, excruciatingly alive. Somehow he perceived a voice in the milky substance, talking clearly and with immense resonance. "Iä, iä. Yogg Sothoth. Nephreu. Cthulhu."

. . . And all that, flashing away. Still dreaming, but now the next dream came to him lucid and so immediate he could taste its pattern. Sheila lay by him, still, absolute, still as rock. His limbs had gathered a terrible energy, felt too light, moved too easily and quickly under his great dry hunger for her. He murdered her. He was confused, the whole time he was killing her he imagined he was making love. And she never spoke, never uttered a sound. . . . The night had increased, it was much later; a shred of moon had driven into the gabled window. The moon looked thin and cheap, like something made of plastic. He was talking, kept murmuring monotonously, his voice thick and deep and full of words he could not distinguish, could not hear. Light poured into the room webby and grimy. It clung to all objects like a gritty gray ash. He kept speaking to her and she would not answer, but in the bed lay a tangle of blood, dark, bluish, in the cheap moonlight. It was streaked, blue, on his forearm and shoulder and chest. It lay tangled with his sperm in the bed; and his body was trembling, evanescent as steam from coffee. He wanted to rise but he kept floundering

back; it was like bathing or drowning. The tall headboard stood over him, a black threshold. Every fiber of
him was sinuous, but frenzied and impotent. His body
suffered agony in the detestable light.

He opened his eyes. Cold with sweat, he stared above
him at the black threshold of the headboard. Sheila
lay by him unmoving but breathing easily and deeply;
sighed once in her warm sleep. He lay for a while
thinking, then turned on his side and went back to
sleep, to dream even more bitterly and heavily.

SIX

The succeeding days widened the strangeness between them. Sheila would hardly speak to him, even averting her eyes as he passed. And he merely passed, going by thoughtlessly, caught up in himself once more, preoccupied with the house. His books and the notes for the monograph on Puritanism lay unused, asprawl after a halfhearted opening of boxes. The house had claimed him, he examined the corners and the walls, finding or seeming to find that the geometry was awry, windows and doors slightly misplaced. He went back to the letters. Peering intently at faint markings under their coatings of dust.

. . . that pece of Land wch boarders on the Mackintosh prop. and probable worth about 500 dols. more or less . . . shamefull incidents talked . . . all the time they talk, one would not think so many idel tonges . . . and even if his religiun is as you clame, no resoun to beleive that he wo'nt break down and come under . . . Sothoth, Nephreu, mabe . . . all in whispers . . .

This day I walked the seven miles to Madison switch-back and made good going of it and found myself in good health, much better than the dr. had intimated to me. Of course took pains to keep well away from Ransom's grove where body of xxxxxx was found dead, and torn in the most awful fashion. Weather delightful even for May, already some of the summer heat is into it. Observed no interesting birds: crows mostly, cardinals, a barn swallow wch I hope will take up residence among us.

Cthulhu [?]. Nyarlath—[?] . . . and will have my SATISFACTON *as i have before this told you . . . will make no diference, he can craul and beg, he can lick my shoes . . .* SATISFACTON—

. . . what rites best employed to bring this about, I do'nt know & must consult. It may be that Stoddard [?] is better informed, certainly the Morgans hold the key to any endeavour of this sort, but are close-mouthed, being the most high adepts. Anyway, it ought to be performed, and although I find myself truly unsuitable, I can only say that, at the least, I am willing and that no one else has come forward. Recognize that it demands a discipline almost intolerable for anyone with a sign of weakness and that considerable bodily pain is involved. I hope mightily that I am equal to the task and that I may live to see it accomplished. If not, there is, of course, no great loss when one weighs what is lost against what may be gained.

. . . this night evermore the darkness Cthu—

He rubbed the dust between his fingers, like a film of oil or sweat, and sneezed. He let the brittle papers fall to the open leaf of the secretary and regarded the loose pile with absentminded distaste. Not a line of them did he understand, hardly a word; and yet he could not stop himself from whittling away hours and days looking at them. "All that nonsense," Sheila would say, had indeed said. He pushed himself away regretfully and went outside.

A clear day, early afternoon. Sheila sat in a kitchen chair at the untended edge of the yard, reading a novel. For a moment he was tempted to go to her, to try to make up to her and trample this silly barrier between them. But pride was still in him, stiff and gloomy, and he would not move. He turned instead to the hill behind the house, going between the house and the woodshed, seeking the open fields.

But he came running back quickly when he heard her shout, shriek.

"Peter! Peter!"

Her book lay tumbled open on the ground. She was standing behind her chair, gripping the back of it, and staring at the ground before her. There a snake was poised, not coiled, not menacing to strike, simply waiting, with round head alift and trembling tongue. It was a dull brown color, about three feet long. Peter found a broken rake handle in the litter at the front of the woodshed and walked, not hurrying, to the edge of the yard. The snake oozed smoothly round—not a ripple in that movement—to meet him. It was harmless, just an errant ground snake.

"It won't hurt you," he said. "Perfectly harmless." He felt unaccountably cheerful.

"Kill it," she said. "I don't care about that. Kill it."

He poked the rake handle at it and it recoiled suddenly. Sheila squealed and gave a little jump backward. "I'm not going to kill it," he said. "There's no reason to. It can't hurt you, and anyway they're good to have around. They eat mice and things." He was unsure of this last notion.

"Will you hush up and kill that thing? I can't stand it. I can't bear to look at it."

"No. I won't. Let me get another stick and I'll carry it . . ."

She tried to lift the chair to strike the snake, but it was too heavy. She pushed it aside and strode forward and snatched the rake handle from his hand. He stepped back automatically, bewildered. She was awkward and frightened; beat the snake behind the head and down the length of it, hitting blindly. It writhed, hissed, twisted, trying to get away but injured now. She dropped the handle and ran away, out to the middle of the yard. Tears rolled on her cheeks, and she was sobbing. "Peter, damn you . . ."

Enraged, he picked up the handle. He was burning angry, regretting that now he had to kill the snake. Two sharp blows precisely on its head he gave it, and it rolled over and over. He got the end of the handle under the twisting body and pitched it down into the weeds. As he came back through the yard toward Sheila he could hear it thrashing about in a drift of dead leaves.

"Why wouldn't . . . You wouldn't kill it because you hate me. You really do. And I hate you too. I hate the sight of you."

"You bitch." His anger had congealed, and was a hot weight in him. His feelings were blunted. He threw the handle spinning into the depths of the woodshed, getting a slight satisfaction from the clatter it made. Slowly he turned his back on his wife and walked deliberately away, going into the house.

Inside he breathed more easily. Confused and dully angry, he walked from room to room, a certainty growing within him. Again in the sun parlor, near the littered secretary, he stopped; stood rigid and still. He recognized the thought that was in him and nodded gravely once, gravely agreeing with himself. And then he put the thought aside and returned almost automatically to the papers which lay there.

—ulhu Iä! Iä! Yogg—

. . . the moon draws wrong has the wrong horn draws wrong has the wrong horn draws wrong has the wrong horn draws wrong has the wrong horn this very night this night evermore this very night evermore this night evermore darkness Cthu—

Had feared that the cows, being alarmed by the Occasion and the pasture already sere in this deathly September, wd. go dry, but have so far maintained their mild, giving 3 or 4 quarts per diem. Some will freshen soon. The sky continues very red at eve (tho' sometimes with green or purplish streaks intermixt) so that the dry weather will probably hold. Mister Peter much concerned with his Chemical researches, very abstracted, the indifferent success of his attempts making palpable effect on his disposition. Gloomy at times, oftimes mistrustful. The weather presently having fretful effect on everyone.

And for a number of nights Peter had kept watch alone, sitting at the kitchen table, smoking his wife's cigarettes one after another—not tasting them—and drinking ugly black coffee that he brewed himself until two in the morning. Sheila had gone to bed long before and slept stubbornly. Then he went up and to bed, but did not sleep; lay wide-eyed in the darkness in the bed apart from his wife, careful not to touch her. He was filled with disgust. . . . And now this night he sat alone again, silently smoking and gulping down the acrid coffee until four in the morning. Occasionally he nodded deliberately, still assenting to himself. Finally he rose and turned off the bare overhead light—there was already a dim light outside—and left the kitchen. He was going to murder her. As he went through the smaller downstairs sitting room, he took the long poker that leaned by the blackened empty fireplace. It was cool and weighty; he was vaguely gratified by the heft of it. He held it forward away from his body, as if he were guiding his way with it like a flashlight. Then through the sitting room and through the long dark hall and, one by one, silently up the stairs.

He paused a moment before the bedroom door, then eased the latch over and let himself in. The air was cool but smelled warm. He found the fuzzy outlines of the furniture, instantly aware of Sheila's muffled form in the bed. She was breathing deeply, sighed now and again in her sleep. He drew near the bed. She was on the other side, scrupulously away from his place, her back turned toward him. She slept, but her body was tense. Her hair gleamed and he stared at it, trying to find the base of her skull. He would like to snap the nape-nerve, to be finished at once.

He struck. She rose from the waist instantly, her eyes wide and unseeing, staring, silent, terrible. She flopped back, roiling, still silent. He struck, he struck.

He had murdered her. The poker dropped. He stood by the bed, regarding it uncomprehendingly, the confused pool, sheet and cold thigh and litter of stain. It had got colder; he clasped his arms round his chest, trying to restrain the trembling of his body. He could not see what lay in the bed, the arc of shoulder and the hair not bright now and the huddle of fouled sheet, but he could not stop staring. He turned, stumbled, going to find his clothes in the dark, and he got them on somehow. He would not turn on the lamp. In the mirrors, even with the light behind him, he seemed hardly there, his body as gauzy as the light, something made to poke holes through. There was a bad smell, rich and chalky. He kept swallowing, but a rancid film stayed in his mouth and throat. He was very cold; now his body seemed capable of feeling only terrifying extremes.

He went out, down the hall, down the stairs, through all the house without feeling his way, his footsteps numb and certain, now his own. The clotted dingy light was everywhere, a grimy dawn was yawning up. He coughed, and spat on one of the curd-colored walls, but his mouth was still adhesive with a clumsy film. He reached the side door and even put his hand on the cold knob, but did not turn it; turned himself instead and went marching back through the downstairs rooms, through room after room, avoiding only the narrow darkened hallway which led to the stairs. In mirrors, glassed doors, cabinet windows his figure appeared, disappeared; and he kept rubbing himself with his palms, as if his body was all a various itch. He did not observe but perceived all the furniture, which perceived him silently, knowing, darkly wise. In the sun parlor he found that he had halted, had turned round and round, stood facing the two whited oblong sister pillows. I SLEPT AND DREAMED THAT LIFE . . . He uttered unresonant laughter, the sound coming flat out of his mouth, inexpressive, hard. Through the glassed door to his left he could make out the heavy squat form of the diseased piano. Again he turned round and round. Then he went through the house once more to the side door and entered to the outside.

Nothing lifted, there was no sense of release, relief. The light seemed no brighter out here, and still hung to him like dank cloth. The sun was not yet up; over the eastern hills was only a lighter grayish smear. The two vertical walnut trees in the lower side yard looked massive and glassy, and the full branches let fall on the lower trunks a dimness—not a real shadow—vaguely shaped like an automobile. He averted his gaze. He went under the dark side of the house out to the dirt road and walked along it for about twenty yards. The prospect was larger, the mountains colorless on the north sky, the nation-shaped fields below him cut through with the smoke-shaped stream, but it seemed no less narrow; it seemed all miniature, enclosing, funneled. In the gray light perched a single gleam of orange-yellow light, steady; it seemed round, but it streaked from the kitchen window of the tenant house. Without hesitation he began to walk the winding descending road, drawn to the single patch of flame on the landscape. He had not thought Morgan would be awake.

He didn't know the time. The hour whitened slowly, but the landscape remained iron-colored, the bad light pervading the dew. Twice he had to stop; he struggled in the wet weeds at the roadside and leaned forward against the bank of the road, clenching the orange clay tightly. He fought to keep the support of his legs. Then he pushed himself into the road again and went along, one numb foot before the other. He got there, paused on the edge of the road above, then let himself down into the yard with a loose ugly shamble. The house looked small now, heavy, squat, diseased. On the tin roof the dew had begun to coagulate, to run off in thin streams. As he went into the shaky eaveless little porch a splash of dew fell on the back of his neck, ran icy under his shirt.

He opened the door, didn't knock, and stood limned there. Morgan was absent. The air was still almost unbreathable, the rancid wood range already cooking, and the flies already industrious, swarming on him immediately. The shaky kitchen table covered by the rubbed dull oilcloth, and on the table the kerosene lamp shedding a glow so yellow and small that it seemed unlikely now he had seen it from the road. Even as he wondered about it, Mina leaned to the screw and turned the wick down, out of sight. The glow was gone. A thread of black smoke rose heavily out of the lamp chimney. They were alone in the gritty sullen dawn light.

Gray in the gray light, her face seemed as impenetrable, as noseless, as he had again and again remembered. Now it was luminous almost, and looked somehow as if it were floating forward. And again her figure, flat and square, without dimension, was all filled with calm waiting, complacent as stone. And again her eyes rested on him, simply remaining still, and he felt enveloped in the gaze; those eyes seemed large as eggs. Her raddled hair hung loose, black as onyx, aggravated the luminescence of the smooth face. —Now in the steaming kitchen he felt hot.

Her voice was soft and thick as cotton. "You're about the worst-looking mess I ever saw," she said. "I never seen such a mess as you are."

He didn't answer, had begun to shudder again. The oily fishy odor stuffed his head.

"You better come here and set down," she said.

78

"You've got a bad case of something, I guess. You sure do look like a mess."

He sat across from her in a creaky little chair, the cane bottom drooping. He slid his hands aimlessly about on the oilcloth.

"You just set there and I'll get you some coffee. It looks to me like you sure could use it. I don't reckon I ever seen anybody in worse shape."

Involuntarily he cowered away. He was sitting by the range. She would have to cross by him to get the coffee. He didn't want her to come near him.

She rose and started toward the stove, but stopped. A slow smile seeped into her inexpressive face. "But it looks like to me you could use something that'd do you more good than coffee. They's a jug back here I'll get. That's what'd do you more good, I bet anything." She turned and went through the door behind her. He heard her displacing a box, rummaging among things which must have been cloth. She returned, holding a gallon jug by its stubby neck, swinging it easily by her side, brushing the black cotton skirt. Her calves were full and muscular, olive-colored. She set the jug on the table, not letting it thump, and went by him to the stove. He twisted away from her, his buttocks clenched tight in the sagging chair. She brought a thick chipped coffee mug back to the table and poured it about half full from the jug. She laughed humorlessly. "I don't reckon a Leland would want to be drinking out of a jug," she said. She put the cup gently before him and turned the handle round toward him. "There you go."

It smelled and tasted oily, of rotting corn. He swallowed it eagerly; and immediately droplets of sweat were on his forehead. He knew absolutely that he was going to be ill, sick to death. He drank again. He had never been more grateful for something to drink.

It was going to be a hot day. Now it was full dawn, and the kitchen was filled with the warm dank religious light, yellow. She stood across the room by the open bedroom door. He felt he saw her with fine clarity, totally, every inch. He wiped his forehead with his blood-smeared wrist. He felt sticky.

ONE

The little house, so humid and rickety—everywhere you stepped the floor gave a little and creaked—was always full of movement. The old man came and went incessantly, God only knew what his errands were. The mother was almost motionless, she moved her great bulk but seldom, and even standing still she occupied much space; sometimes it seemed to Peter that the air of the house and the movements of body and mind of all the others were loaded by her presence, that somehow she affected even his blood. Mina was always coming and going too, she came to Peter and went away. "I got to look after you," she said. "Somebody's got to take care of you."

He lay in the shabby shaggy bed in the little room that seemed mostly a storeroom. Or he would wander from room to room, keeping away from the windows and open doors; and then he would return to Mina's bed and sit straight, holding his knees with his hands, watching with fixed gaze the unchanging splotched op-

83

posite wall. He kept drinking; he had not halted in the three weeks—was it three weeks now?—he had been here. Mina kept bringing moonshine to him, wearing on her face an impassive but still wearily sardonic expression. He loathed the oily raw taste of the stuff; he gulped it quickly and breathed with his mouth open. At night she bore him down in the torn greasy quilts and made love: silent as standing water. It was he who might cry out, her fingernails in him and her cold cold teeth on his shoulder and neck and face. He struggled desperately not to make a sound; when he did groan, his throat hoarse and tight, he was able later to persuade himself that he had made no sound. Mina was relentless as cold wind, she had no feelings, no passion; she seemed to perform with a detached curiosity.

He was continually in a clear acid delirium. Things leaped forward and would get brighter, so clearly he saw them. The unsteady table, the chipped dull blue porcelain coffee pot, the barred iron bedhead, all had outlines strong and burning. Now he lay in the wadded quilts and thought of her father, his face round and red. If you suddenly jabbed him with a pin behind his ear, wouldn't his face pop and go to shreds like a balloon? He drank, and speculated that if you grasped a man's mouth by its corner, you could rip away his meaningless little grin and expose to daylight the real expression on his face. And what would it be? Disgust? A terrible pitiless joy? Anything at all? But it couldn't be done, the grin was too greasy to get a grip on. He drank quickly and regretfully. Or at times he would suddenly find himself on his knees, holding the bars of the bed's footboard as tightly as he could. "Our Father who art," he would say. "Our Father, Our Father, Our Father, Our Father." He could get no further. He would bang his head against the bars until broad red welts appeared on his forehead. And then he would sweat and roll like a pig on the floor. Now tenderly he felt his cheeks; his face must be all ravaged with his own beatings and with Mina's cold teeth. He didn't need a shave. He couldn't remember shaving. Had Mina shaved him? Nausea rose in him to think of her standing with a razor at his face.

Or he would talk, feverishly but clearly; he would actually hold forth with true brilliance, he thought. He spoke about the tragic inevitable division between the cultural aims of a civilization, any society whatever, and the aims of the religion which that culture included. He told how he had at last come to recognize the necessity for a diseased temperament in the understanding of any religious code. He slapped the table softly with open palm. "It's only through suffering that one comes to realize this," he said. "Only through the purest, most intense sort of suffering." He wagged his head gravely. "That's how I have come to know the things I know." At these times he felt he was sixty-five or seventy years old, and a benevolent paternal feeling washed through him; he felt oddly protective of people. They would watch him with slow eyes and stolid expressions. He would expound elaborate theological justifications for suicide, for extreme poverty, for every emotional and physical excess. Sometimes he merely sat in the broken stained stuffed chair in the living room and stared into the tiny fireplace, where lay yet the powdery ashes of the last fire of the winter. He would mutter continuously to himself then, but he wasn't certain what he was saying. It seemed to be a long disquisition on the nature of fault, whether it was ever entirely personal. But he would suddenly break off and shout for help, for it seemed to him that he had become very small and that he lay smothering in the pinkish-gray ash. Mina would come in and press his shoulders into the chair with her cold dark hands. "Hold on there," she said. "You're all right. You just hold on there." She kept her face steady above his so long that he couldn't avoid looking up into it. And then he couldn't look away, and he was awed into silence. Into this unending monologue would creep nonsensical words, words he did not know, an unknown language of despair. "Yogg Sothoth . . . Cthulhu . . . Nephreu . . ." Then his mouth tasted bad, and he would drink again.

It was early July; it was scorching. In the fields the weeds—there didn't seem to be any crops growing— drooped lank and fat in the sun, and there was the continual sawing of insects. Sunlight was hot and heavy in the air, and the tin roof banged like firecrackers sometimes, expanding in the heat. For a while there was no rain and the road was muffled with pinkish-yellow dust, which would rise in long tall plumes as cars passed and then settle, coating the leaves of the weeds and bushes. At night it was cooler and quieter; the crickets sang, but

86

the darkness made the sound seem distant. Then he heard the stream running below and the infrequent splash of something small and dark entering the stream. He hoped it was one of Morgan's muskrats.

Visitors were incessant, and Peter kept out of their sight as much as possible, where he could collect himself. They were mostly farmers, large taciturn men with large weathered rancid faces. He was startled to think how long it had taken him to realize how Morgan made his real living: he was a bootlegger. Somewhere on the farm his still was smoking away, digesting and distilling corn. He was even rather amused to think that Morgan must have to buy the grain from some of his customers; he certainly didn't grow the stuff himself. Was it a profitable business, was Morgan—for all his outward poverty—actually a wealthy man? This thought too was amusing. And now he could account for the endless supply of the alcohol that Mina was fetching him.

But he didn't like it when on some evenings there would be six or seven of Morgan's customers gathered in the hot kitchen. Then he didn't move, but lay stock-still in the raddled quilts, frozen like an animal trying to camouflage itself. He had to guess the number of them from the guttural muttering he heard and the occasional solemn clomp of a heavy shoe. Often enough there were furtive wheezy giggles uttered, and sometimes there was a single voice shouting, not words, but merely a sound of . . . of . . . of fearful surprise, of quick pain, of pained delight. None of these kinds of sounds, and maybe all of them together. What? He struggled to imagine what Mina was doing in there among them. It would be Morgan's idea, that Mina would encourage the men to drink. But he would not find out, he would not move to look. She would come in now and then to check on him, to bring him liquor if he needed it. She would toss a quilt over him and tuck it tightly and contemptuously under his chin. Her blouse would be unbuttoned at the top and when she bent over the bed he observed her small thick inexpressive breasts. Her skin would be warmer than usual from the heat of the kitchen, but it was still cool.

The next day there was a long massive July storm. It was the first time the light hadn't seemed unbearable to him and he had gone out onto the narrow back porch which ran the length of the house. A cool wind, and the yearning stirring of the wild cherry tree below the house, the limbs asway; flies swarmed out of the wide air and gathered on his face and arms, and he didn't brush them away. He sat in a slouched slat-bottomed rocking chair and moved nothing but the forefinger of his right hand, with which he tapped his knee slowly and steadily, in time to a rhythm by which he felt the storm was gathering. Very gradually he accelerated his tapping. Dark gray on gray: the sky was bunching its muscle; it was slow and broad as dreamless sleep. There seemed miles of air between the big first drops of rain. Then it was all loosed at once, noisily drenching the tin roof. The first stroke of lightning was blinding; it seemed that the nearest western hill cleft open, the lightning ascended the skies like something scurrying up a crooked ladder. There was no warning rumble, the thunder issued immediately all in a bang. He dropped to the worn boards of the porch on his hands and knees, heaving and shuddering like a shot dog. Momentarily he imagined the air full of electric particles; if he breathed, his lungs would be electrocuted. Then he was up and ran stumbling into the darkened living room and stood by the fireplace, clutching the daubed stream rock with both hands. He turned round and round. Then he put his hands in his pockets and walked quite casually to the corner of the room and pressed his shoulders against the walls, pressed his face hard into the corner. He kept quivering, but he felt that now it was all right to breathe. When Mina passed her damp fingers along the back of his neck he didn't move at first, but then turned around suddenly, his eyes unseeing and his face blanched. She grasped his shoulders and steered him into the stuffed chair before the fireplace, and he sat there watching it, turned away from the murderous storm. An inky ooze spread on the walls of the fireplace, the rain running down the chimney sides, and an occasional drop fell straight down the chimney, fell into the powdery ashes with a sound like someone letting out his breath suddenly. He gave no sign that he observed anything.

Later he had calmed a great deal, but was very voluble and seemed joyfully excited. The storm had gone away, but trees and the roof were letting down the final drops. The landscape burned with the reflected sunlight. "Look," he said, "look, it's true what they said, that

God does speak to you out of the storm cloud. I was sitting there, and my ears had never been more closed. It came to me when I was sitting there that I was dead, as dead as anyone buried in the ground. It seemed to me that I would like to struggle to come alive again, to make myself alive somehow, but I didn't know how. Even if I knew how I wouldn't have dared, I didn't have courage, I didn't have the strength to find courage. God spoke through the sky to me, and then I was dead, but I came back to life. I had to be killed first, you see, truly killed. The trouble was, you know, not that I didn't have courage to come to life, but that I didn't have courage to be truly dead. I had to accept that I was dead before anything good could happen like that for me. And then when it thundered I knew I *was* dead, and I remained dead for a long time. Whole ages passed while I was dead—I just vaguely knew they were passing. I was in a void, you know, I was where it was all darkness and empty space. Then at last I felt the breath of God, I actually felt it." He ran his fingertips gently, reverently, across the back of his neck. "Here, right here. I literally felt the breath of God pass over my neck."

Mina held him folded in her slow gaze. "That was just me," she said. "I was just trying to get you to pay some mind."

He appeared not to have heard her. He smiled in painful bewilderment. "But I can't remember the words," he said. "Not exactly, anyway. Not the exact words. . . . Isn't it strange that I should forget the words? I can remember all sorts of other things, and none of that is important now. It's very strange, don't you think?"

"Anyhow, you're okay now," she said. "I guess I better get you something to drink."

He shook his head, absently impatient. "I want to think," he said. He felt he was on the verge of remembering, if not the words he so badly needed, then something equally important, a revelation.

Mina went off; she smiled carelessly. He sat where he was and slowly, helplessly, watched the bright event flicker in his mind and go out. For a panic moment he couldn't remember even the flavor of what had happened to him; but something at least seemed to come back, and he felt happy again. Now he was sure that an important event had occurred, something happy and eminent. That was enough. You had to be happy with what you got, he thought. No use expecting too much, it wouldn't be handed to you on a platter.

He rose and went to find Mina in the kitchen. "I think that was a good idea you had about having a drink."

She stood with her legs apart, her hands on her hips. "You reckon?"

"Yes." He chewed his upper lip.

"I don't know about that," she said. "I don't see why I always got to be hauling liquor to you, just whenever you want. I don't hardly see no good I get out of it."

He looked at her uncertainly. "Well . . ."

"If I was to expect you to look after me hand and foot, you wouldn't be doing it, I don't reckon. I don't see the good I get out of it at all." She gazed steadily on his face.

"Well . . ." A slight perspiration came on his forehead.

She put her fingertips against his chest and shoved him backward lightly. "You better go and sit down," she said. "I'll bring it to you, I guess, when I get a chance."

He went back and sat waiting, sadly puzzled. What made her act like that, anyway? What had he done? He rubbed his left side slowly and thoughtfully with a vague circular movement. Lately he had a recurrent pain, sharp at times but mostly a blunt heavy ache, and now it seemed to have settled there. The room was much too bright; there was too much light outside, as there always is after a storm has cleared.

In a while she came, bearing a quart Mason jar of the slightly yellow alcohol. No glass or cup this time, he would have to drink it from the jar. "There you are then," she said. "Is there anything else I got to do to keep you satisfied?" When he looked up at her his face was unknowingly appealing. But she had no mercy.

He wiped his mouth and drank. It was too warm, almost hot, and his stomach surged in an effort to reject the stuff, but he made it stay down. He clenched the jar tightly with both hands and a few drops sloshed on his soiled shirt, a shirt stiff and filthy. The ridges of the edge of the jar rattled against his teeth. He felt better now, but had cleanly forgot the whole day, everything that had happened. It was gone from him immediately and silently, so that he sat drinking blankly for a time with no sense of loss. He was very tired. And then the feeling of having forgot something important began to gnaw in his mind and he became uneasy. He set the jar on the floor and began to rub his face with his hot palms. His chest and legs began to itch too and he scratched energetically. He shifted his feet about and tipped over the jar. He looked at it stupidly for a moment and then jerked down to set it upright. The oily liquid oozed slowly over the worn floor, and the odor of it rose all about the chair, surrounding him entirely, a heavy invisible curtain. There was only about an inch of it left in the jar and he swallowed it down quickly, as if it too might be lost to him. Then he held the jar languidly, and empty tears came into his eyes and rolled down his face. He was motionless, not sobbing, but hopelessly weeping and weeping, without sign of surcease. He was so stupid, so stupid. She wouldn't bring him more after he had wasted it; she was implacable. Maybe he could keep her from knowing about it. And as soon as he thought, he was getting his shirt off. He was on his knees, trying to soak up the liquor with his shirt, which became black and smelly instantly. He turned to wring it out in the fireplace.

"Now what is it? What do you think you're doing now?"

He jumped to his feet, dropped the wet shirt on the chair. He shook his head mutely.

"Get that goddam thing off the chair," she said.

"What kind of a mess have you made now?" She was calm as ice, her voice expressionless.

"Nothing," he said.

"You ain't been getting sick, have you? Is that the kind of a mess you're trying to clean up?"

"No," he said. "It's nothing."

She came closer. "Oh. You've went and spilled that shine I brought you. What did you want to do that for? You was the one wanted it yourself. I got no call to go hauling liquor around for you."

"It was an accident."

"You don't make no sense to me, did you know it? I can't hardly get no sense out of you at all."

"I'm sorry about it. I didn't mean to spill it."

"It ain't hardly the craziest thing you ever done, now is it? You ain't been doing nothing but crazy things around here. It's enough to drive ever' one of us crazy. And look how you was mopping it up. What are you going to wear for a shirt now? Or didn't you think about that?"

He was still holding the soaked smelly shirt. He looked at it mournfully. "I don't know."

"I don't think you got anything to know *with*," she said. "You ain't got no brains, that's all."

He grew sadder; it was clear she wouldn't let him have any more to drink.

"Let me tell you what I want you to do with that shirt. You take it in there in the kitchen and put it in the stove. I don't want to see no such of a mess as that

94

around here. You go on and do it." When he got to the kitchen door she said, "I guess we'll just have to put you on a water ration."

He went on in. He couldn't find the handle to insert into the stove eye to lift it. He opened the high shelf on the range and took out a table fork; reversed it so he could lift with it.

"Now what do you think you're doing?" She had come to the doorway.

"I couldn't find the handle for it."

"What? I can't hear for you mumbling like that."

"I couldn't find the handle," he said.

"It's right there on top," she said.

"Oh." He put the table fork back and got down the handle and lifted off the eye. A few coals were live in the bottom of the firebox. He stuffed the shirt in—it didn't seem likely that it would burn—and set the eye back. He got the handle out and held it, a curious warm cast-iron thing, the tip of it shaped like a square-toed shoe. He imagined hitting Mina with it; he would put blue and red streaks on her face, he would make blood come.

"You just better not, buddy boy," she said. "You better not even think about it. You just put that goddam thing down and come on back here. I sure would like to know what's got into you. You're the craziest damn thing I ever seen. Go on, I said, and put it down."

He hesitated no longer, put the handle on top of the shelf and came to the door.

She was back in the living room, regarded him with cold amusement. "There ain't nobody in the world would be afraid of you no more. You couldn't hurt a cat, and you can just go on pretending all you want but all you can do is just make trouble, make a little mess here and there. That's all. Nobody is going to take you serious." Again she came to him and put her fingertips on his bare thin chest and pushed him lightly backward. "I guess the best way I can think of to keep you from making trouble is just to put you in bed and let you drink. I don't guess you can bother anything there but yourself." She pushed him again. "You go on and get in the bed. I'll be there in a minute and baby you."

He went. He sat on the bed and stripped off his shoes and socks and pants, and then lay back wearily, wearing only his soiled underpants. He lay on his side and tried to go to sleep, but his nerves were acrawl with tiredness and unreleased anger, and he didn't want to close his eyes. He breathed hoarsely. Then she came in, carrying another of the endless jars of corn whiskey. "Here," she said, "and if you spill this or make a mess it's the last of it you'll get to drink in this house, I can tell you. I got more things to do than keep putting up with you." She set the jar on the floor by the side of the bed, and as she straightened she looked flat into his eyes. "I mean it," she said. Then she left, closing the door firmly behind her.

He waited a few moments, until his breathing had slowed. He tried not to think how much Mina had begun to frighten him. Why was she like that? He had done nothing to her, not really. He leaned and took up the fruit jar. Gray and white, but slightly tinged with yellow, Sheila's pert face looked at him through the whiskey. She was smiling: a fixed stiff smile. His hand shook; her face wavered. He was doing well, only a few large drops splashed on his belly. She was smiling. He turned the jar around and peeled the wet photograph off the side, where Mina had stuck it. She had taken it from his wallet. Now he wished he had hit her, that he had made the blood come. Sheila's face was draped between his fingers, the paper all limp, wet. He felt that no one had ever been so abjectly miserable as he; and he let his head roll on his chest from side to side. The photograph wouldn't come loose from his fingers; he shook his hand hard again and again. But he was still extremely careful. He didn't spill any more of the liquor, he had to preserve himself somehow. Finally he wiped the photograph off on the quilts, as if it were a sort of filth which soiled his fingers. Then he leaned and set the jar down carefully, and then lay back, still, his arms along his sides. He began to moan, and it got louder and louder. It got louder, and it didn't sound like a moan any more. He was moaning like a cow gone dry; moo upon moo, and he couldn't stop it. He might have gone on for hours.

But Mina came back in, came straight to him. "Hush up," she said. "Hush up that goddam noise." She slapped his face hard. "Just hush up now." She slapped him again, harder this time, and he heard mixed with his own hollow fear a tinny ringing sound. He began to

97

breathe more steadily, and the noise subsided to a moan. She slapped him once more, not so hard now, and turned away. "I'm goddam if you just wouldn't drive anybody plumb wild with all of your craziness." She went out.

He lay moaning for a while, and then managed to collect himself. The photograph was in wet bits, tangled in the quilt. He began to console himself with the jar.

Or there were times he would be gently melancholy, even rather humorous; would smile sadly but not bitterly and speak in a calm even voice. "The *lachrimae rerum*," he would say. "There's something in the part of a landscape you can see from a window that gives you the clearest idea of what Virgil's phrase really means. The way the window limits the landscape, you know; it intensifies the feeling of being able to see the universe in miniature. Which is what you do when you think of those two words, though I don't think you do it consciously at all. But in the back of your mind somewhere there's a real picture of the smallness of physical existence, of its real boundaries; and there's a corresponding sense of the immensities of the void, of nothingness, which encloses physical existence and to which it really belongs. And then to include the human personality, oneself, in this small universe is to see oneself really minuscule." He chuckled softly. "It's all a question of proportion, you know."

"You're as full of shit as a Christmas turkey," Mina said.

He nodded and smiled gently. He felt very old. "I

don't mean to bore you," he said, "but I know I am. But you can see—can't you?—how hard it is for me to keep my mind alive, to keep it going. With the weight of the circumstances, well, with the way I am now, I feel I've got to keep my wits about me somehow. I know these are nothing but foolish empty speculations, but it begins to seem more and more that my mind won't operate on the material that's given it. The things that happen more and more don't mean anything, and I can't make them mean anything. And as limited as my life has been—and it's always been severely limited—I was always able to make something useful out of a few events. By 'useful' I guess I mean intellectually edifying or . . . or morally instructive. That's what I mean, in fact: every event that happened to me was a moral event. I could interpret it. And now I can't. It seems to me that a morality just won't attach any more; events won't even attach to each other, no one thing seems to produce another. Things are what they are themselves, and that's all they are. Or maybe I'm just troubling myself to no end. One of my troubles always, too many useless scruples."

"Scrooples," she said.

She had got his checkbook from somewhere, and she got him to sign all the checks, blank. He didn't hesitate; it couldn't have mattered less. He felt a detached mild curiosity about the purposes to which she would put the money, but he didn't question her. He knew she wouldn't have told him, and anyway he had no use for it. What could he buy? He himself had been sold, sold out.

The days got hotter. The weedy field below was noisy with grasshoppers. The sun was white as sugar and looked large in the sky.

Sometimes he was very depressed, kept a strict silence. He thought of suicide, thought of slashing his wrists. He pictured his long body lying all white and drained. Perhaps there would be a funeral for him in the brick house, in the dark disused sun parlor there, his body lying in a soft casket beside the disordered piano. But he knew that that was all wrong. There was no doubt he would be cast just as he lay into an open field and left to ferment in the sun. Muskrat food. Yet this seemed appropriate; it was, after all, a proper burial, wasn't it? He wouldn't expect any more than this for himself. In fact, he would stop expecting.—It would take him entire hours to think through a daydream like this, and then he would be mollified but sullen. His body would feel too heavy.

And in the bed too she was relentless. He came away nerveless and exhausted, his face and neck and shoulders aching with the cold bitter hurt. Why, why? Whatever she wanted there finally, it was nothing his body could give, poor dispirited body. She was not satisfied; even blood, he discovered, would not satisfy her. What was it she wanted? How could such stolidness be so demanding? He burrowed against her, spent his last, came fighting for breath. His heart would feel ready to burst; convulsed, convulsed. And it was unhealthy, the whole business.—Or afterwards he would fall into a deep sleep and dream bad dreams which once again he could not remember; but felt in his sleep still the fishy breath of her and the oily taste of her skin.—Or he would have one of the blinding headaches, his mind riven like a stone with the pain. What was it she wanted? There was nothing left.—He would not admit that he cried out in her grip.

After dark the visitors would come again, every night of the week. This time he was drinking in the living room, and Mina let him stay there, didn't lead him through to the bedroom. She closed the kitchen door. He sat in a stupor in the soiled chair and heard without listening the shuffle and thump of the big shoes, the muttering. Finally he rose and went out on the back porch. It was cooler than he'd thought and stars of the deep summer were spread all over the sky; no moon. The night smelled good, snug odor of weeds and flowers and field earth and the cool smell of the running stream. It was the first night he had been outside, and going down the bowed wooden steps he felt slightly elated. He stretched out his arms; he felt he had forgotten until now the feeling of bodily freedom; it was as if a woolen musty coat had been snatched from him. He wandered about in the sparse lower yard, swinging his arms, and looked up at the stars, held still as if tangled in a net, among the small leaves of the wild cherry tree. A faint breeze moved the branches and the stars moved too, seemed to jiggle quietly.

He went round the right corner of the house, going up toward the roadbed. The light from the single small lamp in the living room—it sat on a small table next

101

to the stuffed chair—fell on him as he passed the living-room window and caused him to appear pink and insubstantial. It was a queer sensation to stand here outside and look into the room he had just come out of. He could almost see himself sitting there in the chair, drawn and sullenly silent. Such a pitiable figure he made, or so contemptible a figure. The quart jar sat by the lamp; he had drunk half of it. He went up into the road, not walking steadily, but sliding his feet before him as if he moved on snowshoes. In the gravel of the road he found two small rounded stones and he held one in each hand, squeezing them slightly, reassuring himself of their solidity, their reality. Then he threw them high away into the field below. The kitchen window framed an irregular rectangle of orange light on the sloping ground, and once more he heard that unfathomable intense cry and was attracted by it to the bare kitchen window.

He stood angled away from view. The room was choked with large forms of men. Along the edge of the table next the window a hand lay asplay in the lamplight. It looked huge. The freckles on the hand seemed large as dimes, the distent veins thick as cord. It didn't look like a hand, but, oversized, like a parody of a hand, an incomprehensible hoax. Against the far wall, by the door to the bedroom where Peter slept, a tall farmer leaned. He was dressed in blue jeans and wore a cotton plaid shirt, the sleeves rolled to his biceps, exposing long bony forearms and sharp elbows. His face was narrow and small for his body, seemed as disproportionately small as the near hand seemed large. His nose was prominent and sharp, but his eyes under the shaggy eyebrows looked shrunken, aglitter with concentration. He gazed fascinated at something out of Peter's view, and he licked his thin mouth with a sudden flicker of his tongue. He rubbed his chin with the back of his wrist. Then he moved forward to the table and took up a jelly glass half filled with corn whiskey and drank it suddenly. It spilled a little from the side of his mouth and darkened his shirt, and as he stood by the table close to the lamp his shadow loomed big and fell dark on the bedroom door. Then he stepped back and leaned against the wall once more; and he had not once moved his fierce gaze from what he stared upon.

Peter wanted to see, but he was afraid Mina would see him. Then what? It would be bad. He had to go all the way back up to the road and skirt round the patch of light. Again he picked up a stone and kept rolling it in his hands. His hands were damp with mounting excitement. What was it that everyone in the world knew but he? There was something grave and black being kept from him, and he could feel how important it was, how imminent, and he was desperate to know. There were two other men aligned against the west wall, by the door to the living room. Both wore bibbed overalls. One, a blondish thickset man, wore a faded red sweatshirt, looked yellow in the yellow light. He too stared—as did his companion. His face twitched and he was almost smiling, but not happily; in anticipation, perhaps, as one smiles involuntarily the moment before a vaccination. The other wore a rough blue workshirt, the collar open below the high bib of the overalls. He was taller and looked older than the other man. Spriggy gray hair lay on his chest. He wore an expression almost as unmoving as Mina's, but his stare was as intensely fixed as the others'. Morgan himself stood by the outside door, his hands in his pockets. His face was red as always, his eyes filled with lazy mischief.

Mina had her back toward him. At first he could not make it out: her dark tangled hair on her shoulders; the blouse loose, obviously open all down the front; her thigh olive and bare beneath the edge of the table. He could not see her waist. She was reversed, sitting backward in the chair, straddled on the short fat man who sat round the other way. Her bare leg swung rhythmically and not idly, and it seemed to Peter that she was singing, singing softly music he could not hear. Astraddle, her leg moving to and fro. She gripped the farmer's shoulders and stared intently into his face; it was the way she treated Peter when she was calming him from one of his bad hours. The red fat face was thrown against the chairback, the mouth was open, and the lips tightened and relaxed like a pulse around the dark cavity; lips were frothy and saliva trickled gleaming from one side of the mouth. And now the mouth began to open wider and then almost to close: a fish drowning in air. Mina's naked leg swung easily but more quickly now. And now the muscles under his eyes twitched, this tic rhythmic also, and the man's breath was a hoarse clatter in his throat. Still gripping his shoulder with her

104

right hand, Mina reached behind to the table without looking. She drew forth a snake which was limp at first and then grew taut. She held it just below its head and it wrapped about her forearm. It was brown and splotched with a darker brown; he didn't know what kind it was. She held it apart from her for a moment and then began slowly to bring it toward the man's face. Below the edge of the table her leg swung ever more quickly. The farmer breathed a big bubble of spit; his breathing was louder now. Mina knew when. In time she brought the snake to his face, rubbed it slowly on his cheek. The mottled body writhed carefully, a slow cold movement of the skin without a catch. The man cried out, but the sound seemed not to come from him, but to fall from everywhere out of the hollow air of the kitchen; the sound totally itself, pure unintelligible feeling. "Iä! Iä!" he cried.

Mina spoke gravely and quietly. "Iä!" She spoke in affirmation.

It was over. Again she held the snake apart from them, and then leaned her head forward and put her mouth to the man's neck. When she straightened, the white oval impress of her teeth was plain to Peter. Her leg had stopped swinging. She unbound the snake from her forearm, just as she might take off a spiral bracelet, and dropped the thing carelessly on the table. There it crawled a moment and then lay still; Peter thought that it might be dead now. She got off the lap of her victim easily—it was like crossing a low stone wall—and stood on the other side of the table straightening her black skirt. She brushed her thighs slowly with her fingers. The drab blouse still hung open all down the front and one small solemn breast peered blindly through the window at Peter.

He stepped back quickly out of the light. He turned his back to the window. They had begun talking again. He went again, avoiding the oblong of yellow light, to the road and came back down into the yard. It felt much cooler now than when he had first come outside. Passing the dimly lit living-room window he glanced inside and then stopped. At first he couldn't understand, but looking more carefully, he saw that it was he himself who sat in the ugly stuffed chair. His gangly body was all angles and still. There he sat, uncomfortably asleep, the quart jar still half filled beside him. He stood looking for a few minutes until it all came clear; then he went on, round the house and up the steps; entered the living room and went to sit in the chair. He arranged his body carefully in an angular repose. It was all going to be a bad dream, one of the terrible dreams which caused the sweat to stand on him unmoving and cold. He arranged himself carefully, according to plan, and almost immediately he fell asleep, breathing easily and regularly, not stirring. He stirred once, only slightly, when that hard inexpressive cry sounded again; a different voice, and this time followed by an outbreak of hoarse laughter.

TWO

In early August Mina found what she wanted. Now the heat was tortuous. The sky pressed more closely than before, the landscape seemed flatter, rolled out before the eye, baked, seamless; in the metal heat the different kinds of plants were not to be distinguished. The great white sun was cluttered with yellow and black specks.

"I got somebody who can drive us," Mina said. "I'm sick of this place. I don't want to hang around here forever."

The short blond boy leaned against the doorframe, relaxed and indifferent. He always had about him a liquid uncaring gracefulness. His arms hung at his sides and smoke rose along his body from the cigarette he held in his fingers with a cool exquisite droop. His name was Coke Rymer. Peter, sitting in the stuffed chair, looked at him. He detested Coke Rymer thoroughly; he hated him. He couldn't remember when the fellow had shown up, yawning, glancing about with

107

watery blue eyes which seemed to take in nothing and yet seemed always observing, observing without curiosity. The dark-streaked blond hair was gathered upward in a stiff greased pompadour and was bunched behind in a shabby d.a.

"Coke here can drive," Mina said. "He can take us anywhere we want to go."

Peter nodded. Why was she telling him? She didn't care what he thought about it; she had given him up, for a while at least. He sat in his chair all day, slept in it at night; had denied himself Mina's bed, or had been denied it. "What good are you if you can't fuck?" she had asked, and the question had no answer, of course. He couldn't care, either; for the moment at least that was one ordeal he was spared. Many things in him were damaged; one thing in him was broken, but he didn't know what exactly, was hardly interested. He had gone stale in the ability to suffer, but was certain that Mina knew it; she would find some way to rouse him again. He could contemplate without rancor long intense days of pain, thought of it dispassionately, as if it were a solid library of books that he had to read through.

"I can drive anything with wheels on it," Coke Rymer said. "Take you anywhere you want to go, honey." He had a thin watery tenor voice which wavered on the verge of a grating falsetto. "Just point me on the road and we're gone."

Peter nodded again. What difference did it make?

"They's some things I got to look after first," she

said. "But it won't be long now." She sidled through the door by Coke and went through the kitchen into the back bedroom. She'd grazed him with her thigh.

The blond boy stood where he was, watching Peter with nonchalant eyes, not moving except to puff slowly at his cigarette, which was burned almost down now. Peter was thirsty again; these last few days that he hadn't been drinking the corn whiskey he couldn't seem to get enough water, made innumerable trips to the bucketed dipper in the kitchen. He rose and went toward the door, and Coke Rymer shifted his stance slightly, setting his right foot in the opposite corner of the door-sill. Peter stopped immediately before him, looking carelessly into the pasty blond face with its fixed smile, a meanly dissembling expression. He was indifferent; it wasn't worth it. He turned about and went out the other door onto the porch, down the steps into the yard.

The heat was impossible; stuffed the air like metal wool, would abrade the skin. The copper clangor of the sun filled his ears. There was no breeze, not a hint of it, not even a current in the air. It was so still and hot he felt a match flame would be invisible here in the open. The roaring heat quite overpowered the sound of insects. Under the rough cotton shirt—it was one of Morgan's which Mina had brought him—his ribs trickled with sweat. He walked into the unmoving shade of the wild cherry and stood looking across the glaring fields to the tall glaring hill beyond.

He heard footsteps on the sagging porch steps and turned. Coke Rymer came toward him through the brassy light. In the heat the blond body seemed to waver like steam, to have less weight than a normal human body. He stopped before Peter once again, still wearing the creepy unmeaning smile. "Was there something you was looking for out here, baby?" He inclined his head gently to one side.

He shrugged heavily. The only thing he noticed was how silly this boy was. How old was he, anyway? He couldn't be over nineteen or twenty, was probably seventeen or eighteen. Merely a beer-joint hood, cheap as a plastic toy; something you could wind up and let scoot across the floor, its movements predictable and dull: before long the stretched rubber that made it go would snap and you'd throw it out. What use was he to Mina? He couldn't see what she saw in him. He began to turn away to go back into the house.

Coke Rymer put a wet hand on his shoulder. "Wait a minute, feller. It ain't polite to go walking off while somebody's talking to you. I don't much like it when people don't treat me polite."

He turned again. "Get your hand off," he said. His voice was drowsy.

"I don't much like people giving me orders, neither. Especially when it's some chicken bastard like you. I don't know what you're doing, hanging around here anyhow. Why don't you just cut out while you got the chance? There ain't nothing to hold you here. If I was you I'd just point myself on the road and get gone."

Without hesitating, almost without thinking, he aimed

110

a kick at the blond boy's knee; missed. His foot caught him on the lower thigh.

Coke Rymer blundered backward a couple of steps. "You're right mean, ain't you? By God, we'll see about that." But in the middle of his speech his voice cracked into a hoarse falsetto, and this as much as the kick seemed to anger him finally. He clenched his fists and held them apart close to his body and lowered his head and charged at Peter like a clumsy yearling.

He was calm as wood, unthinking. Again he didn't hesitate, but stepped forward and brought his elbow up fair into Coke Rymer's face. It jolted through his arm like an electric shock, but he disregarded it. This sort of pain was meaningless; the whole struggle was meaningless. It was simply one more task he hadn't asked for but which he had to get through.

Again Coke Rymer staggered back. Peter had clubbed him on the forehead. The yellowish skin reddened, but Peter guessed that it wouldn't bruise or cut easily. "You . . . son of a bitch." He was gasping. Peter could almost feel in his own lungs the weight of the heat the boy sucked in. He came at Peter again in exactly the same way, but then stopped short and threw an awkward punch with his left hand, catching him on the biceps.

He was surprised at the lack of force in the punch and, without bothering to guard himself, stepped backward. Coke Rymer came on unsteadily, and they began circling. In the intense heat it was like fighting under

111

water. Coke made innumerable foolish feints with his fist and kept gulping the hot air. Peter backed slowly, keeping his eyes dreamily over the boy's left shoulder. Somehow that seemed a very clever strategy. He could draw the kid off guard and step in when he pleased. He was momentarily delighted. The mechanics of this struggle, inept and silly as it was, had begun to interest him. He felt a paternal pity for the boy, for his stupidity and awkwardness; it was too bad how he was floundering himself to fatigue out here in the heat. Surely this boy ought to be smarter about fighting than he was. He was still backing, and now he made a feint himself; stepped forward and flicked a short left jab.

He had surprised him. Coke Rymer hadn't been touched, but stumbled over his own feet and fell backward, rolling in the dust. He came up breathing hard, his tee shirt caked with the reddish grit. Lips apart, he breathed through dark crooked teeth. He looked warily about him and again assumed his ludicrous boxing pose.

It was too much. Peter giggled, then laughed hard. He smiled at the boy, fondly amused for the moment. He turned abruptly and walked toward the porch steps, and would have gone back into the house if he hadn't heard Coke Rymer come stamping after him. He looked and ducked; began backing again slowly and carefully. The knife was shining in Coke's hand; the boy held it loosely but confidently. This was different, he could kill him with that knife, he was that silly. Peter felt completely at a loss, kept his balance gingerly and made himself stop looking at the weapon. Where had he read that you mustn't look at the knife but at the man's eyes instead? Some stupid crime novel probably. He wasn't at all certain that it was a wise policy. Out here, even in the broad light, Coke Rymer's eyes were all iris; the pupils had diminished to mere dots. Now he was frightened. He remembered the boy's queer clumsiness and thought of it as his only advantage; he was backing slowly and weaving, careful to keep his balance. He tried his former tactic, stepping forward suddenly and feinting a jab, but it was a mistake. Coke Rymer leaned out casually and pinked him in the left shoulder. He jumped away and began circling again. The cut itself hadn't hurt much, but in a few moments it began to sting; he hadn't realized he'd been sweating so hard. He took a quick peep over his shoulder and then broke and ran, ducking under the floor beams of the porch.

The space under the house was wedge-shaped, the building resting almost on the ground in the ascent of the hill, stilted up on crooked log lengths down toward the west. It was dim and silent under here but not cool. The air was no easier to breathe, stuffed with dust, stagnant. His body remembered it as the air that had stuffed the black attic room before. He ran up a little way under the house and stopped and turned. He couldn't see about him yet; he watched the open space beneath the porch where Coke Rymer would come through. Casual appearance of legs in the blue jeans with the broad glass-studded leather belt, the soiled tee shirt. He heard the boy giggling furiously.

"Why don't you run one time, you bastard?" Coke Rymer said. "I'd just like to see how good you can run." He broke down into giggles. He held the knife at his side, then began carelessly whittling at one of the porch steps. "If you think I'm going to go crawling around in there after you, you're crazy as hell," he said. "That ain't my way, to go crawling around under a house for some chicken bastard. No sir, baby, I just don't cotton to it. Me, I'm just going to wait right here till you come out." He jabbed the knife into one of the log supports and let it remain, near at hand. The sound of his high voice under the house was hollow, had an unearthly whistle in it. "I'll wait right here, me, if I have to for five years. And when you take a notion to come out I'll cut your ass good." More giggling. Slowly the boy took a pack of cigarettes from the pocket of his jeans and lit one.

Except for the open end of the porch the space beneath the house was sided with raw boards which let streaks of light between them. His eyes were becoming accustomed to the dimness. He was half bent now and to get comfortable he would have to squat; he didn't want to do that, he didn't want to see that yellow fixed face. The dust was thick, came almost to his shoe tops. He maneuvered about a bit, trying to find a measure of comfort, and glass snapped under his foot. Looking, he saw bits of a broken Mason jar.

"I'd sure like to know what the hell you think you're doing under there," Coke Rymer said. "There ain't no

114

way out for you, sweetheart, except just by me. Why don't you just face it?"

He moved to his left and squatted. Now the boy's face was hidden by the porch steps; visible were a blue knee, a hand laxly holding a burning cigarette, the knife protruding from the log support. He waited to grow calm again, to steady his breathing. He thought of trying to get out, going quietly and keeping the steps between them, but he knew it was no good. The boy, standing, would see him; he wouldn't get halfway down into the yard. But if he waited here long enough Mina would stop them. Surely she wouldn't let the blond boy kill him. . . . But why not? What did he know about her, anyway? She was unfathomable. The simple fact that she countenanced Coke Rymer at all was unfathomable. All her motives were buried under the ocean. He sighed.

Moving to the left still, still trying to get out of his sight every part of Coke Rymer and the knife, he struck with his foot something solid and metal. At first he couldn't find it, buried in the deep dust. He dug in and dredged it out: a handle for a water pump. It was lovely, it was about two and a half feet long, dull iron. It had a very slight S curve and the end of the handle was smooth, his hand fitted it perfectly. The opposite end of the handle tapered to a flat iron plate which contained three quarter-inch holes evenly spaced. He imagined how the holes would whisper when he swung the weapon. It fitted his hand perfectly, it was proper.

115

He held it before him, admiring the heft and the subtle curve of it. Suddenly in love, he wagged it before him.

Now he could go out. He could keep the steps between him and Coke Rymer—if he could just move silently under the house (the dust would muffle the noise)—and he could come out standing and ready to fight. He went forward on his knees and crawled toward the light. He pushed the pump handle gently along before him, breathed shallowly and quickly, not wanting to sneeze with the dust. When he reached the edge of the house, he took a ready grip on the handle, then rose slowly to a crouch.

The boy was talking again; he talked a great deal, Coke Rymer. "I'm telling you, sweetheart, I don't mind waiting five years for you to come out if I have to. I got all the time in the world." He stooped and flicked the live cigarette butt under the house, into the dust.

Peter came out immediately; his eyes had got used to the light. The boy heard and turned, plucking the knife from the log with the quick careless movement one would use in striking a match. They stared at each other over the descent of the sagging steps; it was a moment or two before Coke Rymer glimpsed the pump handle. "What's that thing you've got?" he said.

He began to edge round the steps.

"That won't do you no good, just a ole pump handle. I got something here can cut your ass good."

But he didn't come forward; kept still, watching the swing of the handle. Was *he* going to duck under the house now? That would be too much; Peter thought he

116

would laugh himself sick if he drove the boy to ground like a rat, as he had been driven. No, now Coke began to sidle away from the porch, going back down into the yard.

"It won't do you no good. I can throw this here knife." Almost without looking, and with the one hand, he reversed the knife, holding it lax between thumb and forefinger about halfway down the blade. But there was no conviction in his eyes, and his voice was again teetering on the edge of a falsetto. Peter jumped forward and poked him in the stomach with the handle, holding it like a broadsword. Not a hard blow, but telling, assertive of his advantage. The watery blue eyes bulged; the yellow face splotched with red.

"Throw down the knife," Peter said. He was surprised; his own voice was whispering and rough. "If you throw the knife down I won't have to knock your brains out."

"Hell you say. I ain't putting this knife down for no son of a bitch. I throw it anywhere, it'll be in your belly."

But surely it was obvious, even to the boy, the superiority . . .

"Go on, go at it. I want to see you kill each other off." Mina, of course. She stood on the porch watching and now began to let herself gently down into the broken rocking chair. She rocked complacently, enfolding the whole scene with her still gaze. "Go on," she said. "Kill each other off, why don't you? Ain't neither one of you worth what it takes to keep you alive. It's

117

been a long time since I seen a good fight. Let's see you do it."

They looked at one another helplessly. Their animosity was smothered completely.

She saw it too and laughed, a hard flat faceless laugh. "And I guess it'll be a good long time before I ever see another good fight, if it's up to you two. You ain't hardly got no fight in you, have you?" Again, the flat hard laugh.

"Aw shit," Coke Rymer said. He stuck the knife listlessly into the porch steps. "I can take care of honeybunch here any time I want to. He don't bother me none, him and his goddam pump handle. I can take care of him without batting a eye."

Peter knew better; he was silent, vowing not to let the handle out of his sight. His life was bound to it now; he could see the connection as simply as if it were a glittering chain, a handcuff which held him to the junked iron. For a while now his life had been bound to iron, and the necessity of the handle didn't surprise him; it was inevitable.

"I don't know whether you can or not," Mina said. "Mr. Leland might be some tougher than you think. What I do know is, you ain't going to try it no time soon. It ain't something I'd just let go on and on. Work to get done around here. We got to get packed up to leave and you got to help get it done."

"That's all right with me," Coke Rymer said. "I'm ready to go any time, anywhere you want to."

Peter was ascending the steps, clutching the iron

tight. It was the only thing solid in him now. His legs trembled, and his empty right hand. The delayed fear in the struggle with the blond boy had settled on him now and his heart staggered in him. His seeing was blurred with fear. He stopped at the porch edge, Mina watching him amused.

"And what do you think you're up to?" she said.

He licked his caked lips. He was careful to look away from her face, over her head into the shadowed sullen air. "I'd like to have a drink," he said.

"I guess you don't mean water then," she said. "I guess you mean you want liquor."

"Yes." He was still not looking at her.

"What makes you think you'd get any? What have you done to get any? Have you done anything for me lately?"

"No." He spoke slowly. "No, but . . ."

"But what?"

His mind was empty. He let his shoulders rise and drop. Helpless.

Coke Rymer spoke, his voice at once belligerent and whining. "I don't see why you want to put up with him. What do you want with some crazy old drunk anyhow?"

"Hush," she said. "Me and Mr. Leland's still got lots of things to do together. Don't we, Mr. Leland?"

He nodded numbly.

"Even if you can't fuck no more."

He nodded again.

She rose easily and came toward him and he sank

119

back in himself, though his body didn't move. Her silvery eyes held the whole range of his knowledge; she placed her hand casually on his penis, withdrew it without haste. "No. Not any more. But there's always something else, ain't there? Why don't you just go and set down in the rocking chair and I'll see if I can't find what you're looking for. Something'll put hair on your chest." She grinned. "Make a man out of you." She stepped lightly away and went to the door and turned. She spoke to Coke Rymer; her voice was sharp and peremptory. "Quit that fiddling around and come on in here. They's work got to be done if we're ever going to get going."

"All right," he said. "I done told you I'm ready to go." He stopped his scraping of the notched edge of the porch step and folded the knife and put it into his pocket. He came up the steps with his buoyant grace and followed Mina into the house, pausing only to give Peter a single swift foul-natured glance.

Peter giggled. That one last glance had so much about it of the impulse of the hindered child who sticks out his tongue. That was Coke Rymer, all right: a spoiled child. Spoiled, soiled; but also despoiling, assoiling. He darkened the heavy brightness of the air, and even in his total blind paleness there was a dimness, as of a furry rot-inducing mold. He tipped the rocking chair forward and back, but the motion augmented the queasiness that his belated fear had brought on and he stopped quickly, sat in the shadowed porch gazing out. The settled heat had not moved. The limbs of the wild cherry tree dropped, the sharp leaves looked buttery in the sunlight. He was simply waiting, and in a while Mina did appear, holding one of the too-familiar jars loosely at the ridged top.

"Here now," she said. "Here it is, you can drink it. But I don't want to see that you've poured none of it out or spilled it or wasted it, or you'll never see another drop from me as long as you live."

She went back into the house. He looked through it at the landscape, which was streaked and crazed and looked even hotter through the yellowish liquid. He began to drink, drank steadily, and within the hour he was delirious and lying on the porch in foetal position, his hands clasped tightly between his knees. He was prophesying in a loud voice, heedless. And then he began to whisper. "Mina's right," he said, and the sibilance of his whisper was echoed in the sibilance of his clothing as it rasped on the boards of the porch. He squirmed on the floor but made no progress. "Mina's right about the snake. We live as serpents, sucking in the dust, sucking it up. The stuff we were formed of, and we ought to inhabit it. We ought to struggle to make ourselves secret and detestable, we should cultivate our sicknesses and bruise our own heads with our own heels. Where's the profit in claiming to walk upright? There's no poisonous animal that walks upright, a desecration. It's better to show your true shape, always. It's better to s— . . ." But now he had squirmed forward, to the edge of the porch, and his forehead knocked against a supporting post. He raised his head and began to gnaw

121

feverishly at the base of the post. The wood tasted of bitter salty dust. He closed his eyes and kept gnawing until the fit had passed off him and then he lay weak throughout his whole body. He was sweating, the bitterness of the post streamed out his pores; and a fine-edged clarity possessed him. He felt unutterably ashamed, and he turned his eyes toward the door, knowing already what he would see, his face and mouth and ears burning with fearful shame.

"Ain't you something?" Mina said. "Ain't you a sight?" She didn't laugh, but turned away and disappeared again.

Grasping the post, he pulled himself shakily upright and shook his head hard, trying to clear it. He staggered to the rocking chair and folded into it and began to drink again. That was Mina's way, that was always her way: she simply appeared and disappeared when she liked, everything was always under her control. He remembered that only a few weeks ago he had daydreamed that when she had finished the life of his body she would have it discarded—dumped—in the fields under the brutal sun. Naked to the corrupting heat . . . Now he realized that he wouldn't be so lucky. That fate had been reserved for his wife's white body; Sheila, whom he had murdered, lay out there somewhere, going to pulp in the southern weather. Trying to turn the thought away, he turned his head, shook it hard again. He didn't have to guess about Sheila; Mina had told him what she had had done, repeated it again and again. Of course. . . . Mina would always do exactly as she pleased. Coming and going, her movements admitted of no prediction, except that she would continually find him in the moments of his worst shame. Now he had guessed that this was her motive in keeping him, to observe how far downward he had gone. He had become a queer experimental animal; Mina used him purposely to try to gauge through him the fiber of the whole species. And he too felt a chilly detached curiosity. How far into this rushing darkness could a man go? When he had devoured his heart, what was there to push the machine along? At what point was this machine no longer recognizable as himself? He glimpsed a blurred moment of illumination: at that bodiless point—whenever, wherever it was—that the humanity in him melted, disappeared, the universe rested. At least one universe, the humane one. In this momentary half-vision (which he could hardly believe he had been granted) he felt obscurely the presence of other systems, other universes, to which humanity—his humanity— was irrelevant. Mocking crowded points of corruscation. Infinite coldness. He shook his head for the third time and drank again, feeling gratefully the flush of the liquor leap upward in his body from his belly.

THREE

They were traveling. They had loaded Peter into the back seat with the same uncaring gesture they had loaded whatever it was Mina was carrying into the trunk of the car. He sat numb while they made the final preparations, overwhelmed by the all-too-familiar look and odor of the machine. It was his car, of course; Mina had taken possession of everything that had once belonged to him and Sheila. No question about her purposes with his possessions; she would waste them totally and carefully. He observed the scratchy ribbed felt overhead, the frayed latticework of the seat covers. Wouldn't it be funny if the dome light worked, now that Mina had the car? It had never once worked when the car was his. He wondered if the little leather-bound copy of the Gospel of St. John was still in the glove compartment; surely Mina would have no use for that. He was still slightly drunk; he sat carefully steady and kept his hands clasped between his knees.

They were simply leaving, no goodbyes. Neither Morgan nor his wife—who was almost never seen in the house—came out to speak or to wave. She and Coke Rymer finished what business they had inside the house (without doubt she bore Coke Rymer, too, desperate down into the rancid quilts) and got into the car. He drove and she sat listlessly, her bare arm stretched along the top of the front seat. She glanced about with a placid curiosity. Peter had none; sat stolid, feeling the pour of warm air on him, heaviness of the moving landscape. Behind the car the reddish-yellow dust rose solid as wood and then dispersed to separate particles. Peter looked behind once to see the tenant cabin tossing, as if swimming away in the yellow haze.

They passed the big brick house, the house of the murder, and Peter turned his head. There, it had loomed before him suddenly round a sharp curve of the road and stood shocking in the glacis of the hill. He turned his head. Even the single glimpse of it disturbed, served to force into his gullet the sour taste of the guilt he had been so long now trying to swallow and to keep down. No specific memory—nothing so acutely defined —but a shapeless huge nausea overwhelmed his nerves, and he kept his head turned. He simply would not remember, he denied it all.

On this road it was farmland all the way. On a board fence bordering the roadway, a large gaudy metallic-looking rooster flapped wings and crowed, too late in the day. The racking crow sounded mechanical. Through the bottom fields the creek wandered, not appearing very different from where it ran by Morgan's cabin. Sunlight burning in ovules on the glassy leaves of poison oak. Two white butterflies involved in hectic acrobatics. The passing in and out of the shadows dropped by massy oaks. Splotched cattle on the splotched hills. Barbed-wire fences, the weathered posts leaning awry, sagging rusty wire. Hot gray roofs of squat chicken houses. Barns red and gray, looking fat and hollow at the same time. The neat white houses and the battered tenant cabins, each garnished on one side with lines of hung washing, spectacular in the breeze. Noise of flung gravel, of wind.

And then they hit pavement and Coke Rymer drove faster. The wind that poured in on Peter cooled and increased in volume. Coke was intent on his driving; he drove savagely but with a flashy accuracy, carefully watching the road before him, though he never seemed to look into his rear-view mirror. Nor did Mina glance into the back seat at Peter. Now and again she would draw her fingers slowly along the top of the front seat; she was caught up in her own listless thoughts, and even the slight curiosity she had at first shown in the passing scenery had vanished. Peter let himself relax; the first motion of the car had made him feel faintly ill, but now he let himself drift with it, tried to enclose the oblique movements of the machine in his body and, lax now, felt that he had partially succeeded. It was not a good car, an old one—it was what he had been able to afford —and it quivered mercilessly and, after a full stop, shuddered alarmingly climbing into the gears. He ought to have got a new car long ago, but there hadn't seemed

126

a real need and, of course, there was the question of money. Even now, he didn't know what the need for the car was. He had no notion where they were headed, except that the direction was easterly, out of the mountains. He didn't even know whether Mina had planned a definite destination. She was perfectly capable of truly aimless movement, he thought, but then he knew the thought was false. Even if there was no destination, her moving would never be purposeless; all her energies were bent to a single purpose, she never swerved. This he had observed again and again—and a lot of good his observation was. What this purpose was he had never fathomed, so that all her actions were mysterious and sometimes seemed almost crazy; but he didn't doubt that there was a single principle which would bring it all to him clear if he once could grasp it. These thoughts made him restless and he shifted his feet on the floor-board, feeling for the solid presence of the pump handle. He touched it with his toe and was grateful and comforted. He glanced down at it, permitted himself a faint smile in the roaring windstream. He planned to take care of the weapon, to polish it till it gleamed, and then—and then a light oil bath to prevent its rusting again. He pondered. And perhaps too, a rubber grip for it; he would need only a few inches from a rubber garden hose. . . .

He felt that he really ought to know Mina's purpose: it seemed so closely dependent on Peter himself. There was a reason, yes, why he had been subjected to what he had. The idea of punishment formed in his mind, but the idea of the crime for which he was being punished would not come. It was not murder—ah, that was a mere word to him now; the memory of Sheila herself had disappeared, to leave only an impression of bright sheeny light, no person at all—no, not murder, but something more terrifying, something previous to anything he could ever remember, previous, he sometimes thought, maybe to his whole life, previous to his birth.

Regular monotony of the passing telephone poles, dark, spearlike. The shadows slipped through the interior of the car like spears. Now racing the candescent threads of railway track which lay along the road. He could follow the progress of the stretched shape of the sun as it zipped on the iron. Impression of heatless light. And then they caught up with the train, passed the red caboose, went exhilaratingly by the rollicking freight cars. He heard them bounding along the track. *Rocker unrocker rocker unrocker.* Passed the diesel engine which let go with its ugly sour horn. Shot through narrow concrete bridges. Up and breathtakingly down dark wooded hills. Coke Rymer was taking the secondary highways; Mina must have asked him to keep off the broad fast interstate system. Again Peter couldn't guess her reasoning; it was no less public the way they were going. Cars came toward them and slipped by, momentary as a wink. Trucks loaded with heavy paper bags of fertilizer lumbered along before them, and Coke Rymer cursed, slowing suddenly; Peter was always certain they would bang into the trucks. He cowered inside himself; imagined smothering under a flood of smelly fertilizer.

They rode on and on. Occasionally they would pull into a nondescript service station for gas, or Coke Rymer would say, "I got to go to the little boy's room," or "I got to powder my nose." His coy silliness, something always grim about it. Mina would go into the station and return, bringing Peter a soft drink and cheese crackers with peanut butter. The cellophane packages were always dusty, he wiped his fingers on his trousers. But he ate and drank dutifully. Four empty soft-drink bottles rolled clinking together on the floor. In one station Peter went to the restroom, and there, in the acrid odor of the disinfectant, looked out the window before him, a narrow slot in the white concrete block wall, and thought absurdly of escape. But there was nothing to escape from. He was not a prisoner, not held by force. He was simply bound to Mina wholly; he was his own prisoner, he could escape by dying, by no other way. He uttered an involuntary sob, zipped his fly, lurched out. The sunlight struck his eyes like a slap.

It got later, the sun was behind them. The eastern sky was orange, wild with queer cloud shapes. Still they went on. The land got flatter, and towns were glimpsed before they were arrived at, the lights making ghostly white aureoles on the horizon. The young men were out, dolled up, restlessly courting the girls. Gay convertibles; shaggy fox tails pendent from radio aerials. One little town like the others, all flat on the landscape like stamps pasted in an album. Sharp brick buildings in the evening light; they looked like biscuits set out of the oven to cool. And yet it all fitted. The landscape was perfectly integral. Across the slim horizontal rows of cotton or cane, the weathered vertical form of the farmhouse seemed truly correct: its gabled porches, its uprightness, its bony angularity. On the whole land a somnolent watchfulness, a waiting for the night, for coolness, for the justice of stars. They passed drive-in movies, and the great flat faces of strangers fluttered away in the darkness; they were quickly oppressive, these visions of bright love and violence, a tipsy staggered glimpse of the secret heart of the land. Peter felt conspicuous and embarrassed at seeing the great screens; it was like peeking into bathroom windows.

It had begun to cool, but he still felt hot. His body was gritty with dust, filmed over with evaporated sweat. The oncoming headlights burned his eyes, scraped on his exacerbated nerves. They kept driving on and on, and he wanted to cry out for them to stop it, to stop it: they were going nowhere, there was nowhere to go. Why couldn't they let up? Why was it so necessary to squash oneself to a handy ball and keep torturing it along over the flimsy landscape? He leaned and picked up the comforting pump handle and held it tightly across his lap. He gripped it hard, not to let go, and the tightness began to seep out of his chest. He ran his finger along the clear curve of the metal; it was he, this weapon; he could punch holes in the world, he possessed heroism kept carefully in check. He settled his head back against the seat. His eyelids flickered. He dozed resistlessly, still gently fingering the pump handle.

In the sharp restive dream he was a spider; no, a daddy longlegs. He scoured in jagged lines over the fields, searching out water with an unerring hunger. His size was protean; grew monstrously; diminished. On the skin of the great water, when he found it, he would drift in coolness, the big overhanging leaves of the weeping willow would keep away the sunlight. The soft fields were singing softly. In the harsh embittering dream was a peaceful dream, of waters shot with healthy shadows, of the rounded spaces under trees enclosing as with cool arms. But in the heated fields his six-legged unstable body was painful, crazy. All his eyes had nowhere to look; a glazed glare held his vision with unbreakable force. He moved crookedly; he did not want to move. There was no reason for it, there was no purpose in it. The six-legged machine was its own volition, and he a prisoner trapped. It came to him that this at last was the true image of his sickness, and in his sleep he was somewhat mollified. The sweat ceased to trickle down his sides from his armpits and his grip on the pump handle gentled.

"All right, honey, you can climb out of there. You've got the place we're looking for."

He was awake immediately. They had stopped. Coke Rymer tugged at his shoulder through the open window. He didn't know where they were. It was full dark and cool. All round the car were trees, sibilant in the night breeze. He clambered out, stiff and dizzy, and raised his head to look at the sky. Random stars pierced the foliage, and the tree limbs moved now to sweep them from sight. He flexed his arms, held them out straight, rotated his neck on his shoulders. He breathed deep, grateful, but when he walked forward he staggered, the stiffness still in his legs.

Mina was leaning against the front fender, resting easily. Nothing bothered her; she knew where they were, why they were here. "I hope you had a good nap," she said. "That might be what you're good for, you know it? Just to sleep. You might could get to be a real expert."

He turned away from her, scratched the small of his back with both hands.

"Or you could drink liquor," she said. "I forgot about that. There's two things you can do, right there."

He wandered away from the car, heading ignorantly into the darkness.

"Where do you think you're going?" Mina said.

"I'll be back in just a few seconds," he said.

"He's going off to take a leak," Coke Rymer said. "Do you want me to go with you, honey? To hold your hand?"

It was dark and cool, and he began to feel better, not so heavy. His body was still sticky with travel, and as he stood to urinate he listened hopefully for the sound of a stream nearby, water to slice away some of the road dust. No sound of water, but a sound, the

132

night breeze hazing the foliage, like water; and even this seemed to help, to refresh. There . . . Now he did feel refreshed, and as he walked back toward the car he permitted himself a vague half-smile, thinking, *I woke and found that life was duty.*

They were waiting, still standing by the car. "We're going to sleep in the back. You can sleep up in the front, if you want to," Coke Rymer said. "The steering wheel gets in the way, that's why."

"All right."

"Or if you want to, you can sleep out here on the cold ground. I don't give a damn what you do."

"All right," he said.

His acquiescence robbed Coke Rymer of anything to say. He stood uncertainly. "Well . . ."

"Oh goddammit, come on," Mina said. She caught the blank boy by the arm and opened the car door and propelled him into the back. "If it was up to you-all, I guess you'd just stand around talking all night. There's better things to do than that." She turned. "Why don't you just take another nice little walk? I don't reckon they's anything around here to eat you up. So all you have to do is just not to get lost. You can take a little walk and watch out where you're going." She got in and closed the door.

He didn't feel that a nice little walk was what he needed, he was tired. But he'd better go. He put his hands in his pockets and started away, heavily desiring alcohol. How much easier the trip would be if there were something to drink. Mina would know that, and yet she had allowed him nothing. . . . He tried to put it out of his mind, but this resolve simply made it all the worse; his very neurons seemed to cry out for the stuff. The breeze had not abated and now it was cooler than he wanted. He hunched his shoulders forward. He walked aimlessly, noticing nothing about him. Now and again he looked up, walking on, and the stars seemed to float backward over the various shapes of the trees. He kept wondering if he had come far enough, if he had been gone from the car long enough to satisfy Mina. Finally he turned back and began to retrace his path. It wasn't difficult here; the undergrowth was sparse, the trees were mostly large and well spaced. Two or three times he wandered off the track and had to extricate himself from patches of bush and briar.

But there was no real trouble, and he got back too soon. He came to the edge of the little clearing where the car sat and there he stopped, hearing Coke Rymer's choked muttering from the back seat. He let himself clumsily to the ground and sat with his legs crossed, listening. Again he let himself smile, irony without joy; and he waited. The low whistling intake of breath he heard, the unnerving muttering: all the cruel mechanics of the lovelessness of the deed. He waited knowingly, certain of what would come. And he heard it: Coke Rymer's anguished last outcry, uttered twice and enveloped in the breezy darkness. Coke too was under the pain of it. Snap. O, her cold cold teeth, the fishy breath of her. It was unremitting and continual; she was relentless. He smiled with solid satisfaction for the first

134

time in a long while. She had no mercy, none. Now it wouldn't be very long before Coke Rymer was like Peter, not male; he wouldn't be able to fuck any more. He would be broken, a figure paper thin. . . . Abruptly he hankered after his pump handle. He should have brought it with him, he felt frightened without it. It was his weapon, and if anyone ever needed a weapon, it was he, for surely there had never been anyone so utterly defenseless, so helpless and so caught in incomprehensible dangerous toils. The land and sky looked upon his helplessness.

What was ever going to satisfy her?

He lingered; waited until what he hoped was a decent time had elapsed—smiled, a third time, because the word "decent" had come into his mind—and then rose, brushed absently at the moist earth that clung to his trousers. He went to the car, walked round the front and opened the door at the driver's seat as quietly as he could. It remained dark in the car, the dome light didn't work, not even for Mina. He looked into the back. Coke Rymer lay squashed against the seat, already asleep and breathing heavily, wearily, through his gaped mouth. Mina lay on the outside, propped on her elbow, taking up most of the room. She wasn't even disheveled. She regarded Peter with her pale, almost luminous eyes; spoke in a level, quiet—but not hushed —voice. "Well, did you have a nice walk?"

"It was all right," he said. There was a glitter of petty triumph in his voice that he couldn't keep out, and he hoped she wouldn't notice it.

135

"Good for you," she said. "Get some exercise, that's the best way to get your strength back."

He leaned in and began to crawl across the seat on his hands and knees. He wanted to have the steering wheel at his feet.

"You know," she said, "it wouldn't bother me none to turn old Coke out of the back seat here. He's just going to sleep like a dead man. If you was to want to come back here and try your luck for a while, I'd roust him out." Her voice was lazy and impassive, her eyes two gray patches. "You reckon you feel up to a little more exercise?"

All his little happiness melted away. "I'm afraid not," he said.

She sniffed; sheer disdain. "I didn't reckon you would."

He lay down, then squirmed around to close the door; got his position back and lay there, sour and painful. He needed fiercely the pump handle, but he was determined he would not ask her for it. He lay awake, holding his genitals in his left hand. But sleep at last caught him, held him silent and dreamless and he woke into the daylight without rancor, feeling rested. But thirsted harshly for Mina's dispensed alcohol.

In the early afternoon they came to Gordon, a town not different, so far as Peter could tell, from the scores of towns they had passed through. The surrounding countryside was flat, and on the easterly breeze was a whiff of brackishness; it couldn't be many miles from the ocean side. Grass struggled to grow here, and the earth was often bare, a pinkish-white dust blanketed over packed burning clay. Here clay land was changing over into sandy land; the two soils melted together. The sunlight too seemed powdery, thick on the leaves of magnolia trees, collected in drifts like burning snow in the upper crevices of boxwood shrubs.

"Well, this here's the town you wanted to get to," Coke Rymer said. "Where do you want me to go from here?"

"Just drive us around a little and let me look," Mina said. "I'll let you know where I want you to stop."

"Well, you're the doctor."

"That's right," she said.

The streets of Gordon were quiet. Cars were parked along each side of the main street, pocketed when it was possible in the shade of tall oak or magnolia trees. Grave-eyed negro children passed on the sidewalks, swinging wet bathing suits by their sides. The houses here were mostly white wooden houses of two storeys, but here and there were small brick duplexes with the silvered boxed air conditioners protruding from the less sunny windows. Through the main square of the town ran two railroad tracks, side by side, and the town was truly divided by them. On the east side of the tracks the moneyed houses began to grade finely down into grudging respectability and then at last into frank poverty. The asphalt pavement narrowed and was broken along the edges. Here were the one-storey white frame houses, held off the naked dusty yards by unpainted concrete blocks.

"You can turn here," Mina said, and Coke Rymer obediently turned left into a red jolting dirt road. The sloping ditches were filled with black cinders, and the houses were no longer white, but stained brown or weathered gray. They were in a negro section, and there were no longer signs at the corners telling the names of the streets. Here the streets were nameless. There was an occasional shabby grocery store, its false brick siding plastered over with advertisements for soft drinks and headache powders.

"Right here, now," she said, and he braked the car, let the motor idle. They had come out of the negro section into a beaten-down poor-white area. On the right was a squat white house, but Mina was observing the house on the left. It was small, looked as if it would contain four rooms or so; the rough oak siding was stained a dark brown, as dark almost as creosote, and the white trim was mostly battered away. The unfenced front yard was as bare and dusty as the others. The roof was gray galvanized tin, no different from the roof of Morgan's house back in the mountains. Peter saw nothing interesting about the place. There were a hundred, a million others which would mirror it without a scrap of difference. . . . But it was what Mina wanted, what she must have been looking for.

"You can turn off the car," she said. "This here's the place we been looking for."

He turned off the motor and they climbed out, leaned resting against the heated metal of the car.

"I don't see what's so wonderful about this place," Coke Rymer said. "Who is it lives here, anyhow?"

"They don't nobody live here," she said. "This is where we're going to live."

The blond boy shrugged, sucked his front teeth. Peter was at first bewildered—it made no sense, none—but then he was grateful. They could move the stuff in the trunk of the car into the house, he would help move it, and then Mina would give him something to drink.

FOUR

When Peter woke, his gangly frame was shuddering all over, not just from the morning cool, but because this was the condition of his awaking body. He struggled with his limbs. The chains clashed and thumped on the splintery kitchen floor. He didn't want to open his eyes. The early sunlight would strike like a bullet into his brain. The smell of slopped liquor, of chewed rancid scraps of food, hung in the room, only slightly freshened by the raw air that poured in. A window was broken or maybe somebody had left the door open. The light was on his eyelids, forming behind them a coarse abrasive red curtain which made his temples ache. An uncontrollable belch brought up the whole fetor of his gut and while he struggled to breathe, keeping his mouth open to dissipate the deathly taste, droplets of sweat popped out over his whole length, dampening his shirt and pants which were already salty and sour from the weeks before. He gasped.

Then he lay still, trying to listen, but all he could

hear was his own thick choked breathing. When he held his breath he could hear only the blood swarming in his ears. But no one seemed to be awake but himself; he had to lie still. If he woke them, moving his chains loud enough to wake them, they would kick him to bits. He tried to place his head, without moving his arms and legs, so that the sun couldn't get at his eyes. It was no good. The day had already begun its dreadful course, the sun was poisoning the sky. He felt the baleful rays sink into his pores. His spine felt as if metallic cold hands squeezed it intermittently. He couldn't get his face out of the sunlight.

He lapsed into a fitful red doze, but was jarred awake by the fear of rattling the chains in his sleep. With her big mouth Mina would tear his Adam's apple out of his throat. She would spit it on the floor and crush it with her big mean heel, like killing a cockroach. He could almost see her unmoving face hovering over his, feel the cold fishy breath of her; her teeth would be like hundreds of relentless needles. He whimpered help- lessly, but stopped it off, constricting his throat like a ball of iron inside. If he began whimpering hard he couldn't stop and it would get louder and louder until the moos came on him, and then they would beat him until he stopped. He stopped the whimper. His chest already felt jagged inside where they had kicked him. He fought to make all his muscles relax from the quivering, and stream on stream of tears rolled down his face. If he opened his eyes the tears would shoot sharp spears through them.

141

But he was so tired he was almost inanimate. He fell into a yellow sleep, bitter with a drilling electric sound and the smell of black mud and fish. He dreamed that he had no face at all and that his eyes were unseeing dark splotches on his gray stony back and that he swam forever through this world of solid objects which were to his body liquid. In the dream there was nothing he could touch, his body was mere extension without knowable presence.

Again he came awake, now with the black thirst upon him. The sunlight no longer filled his face, and yet he did not think that he had slept long. He felt a warm presence. At first his eyes wouldn't open, and he thought that they had clicked them shut forever with locks and he thrashed around, beginning to whimper again, not caring about the chains now. He got his eyes open, though they were still unseeing, but it was hard to breathe. He blew his breath out hard and an inexplicable chicken feather blew up and stuck on his cheek. He gagged. Then when he could look it was all dim, but behind the dimness was a bright white ball with the hurt strained out of it.

He could not think any more. Everything in his head was gone. At last he realized he was looking at the sun. It shone through the dark gray cloth, reddening faintly the stretched muscles of the legs which arched over his face. He knew them already, Mina's plump steady legs, taut curve at calf and thigh, arrogant, careless. He looked up the pink-tinged insides of her legs. He knew he had always been right. There at the X of here where her woman-thing ought to be was a spider as big as a hand, furred over with stiff belligerent hairs straight as spikes. He couldn't stop looking. His gullet closed and his chest began to strain for air; he could hear it begin to crackle. His throat opened again, but it was hard to breathe because the whimpering had started. It started loud and he knew there was no hope stopping. The moos had got to come now; and then they would kick him to bits.

"Hush up, just hush up," she said. "Can't you never take a joke?" With the hand which wasn't holding up the front of her skirt she reached down there and plucked the spider away. She held it free above him and though he could see it was only a toy, only wire and fuzz and springy legs, he couldn't keep the whimpering back. It got louder; the moos had got to come.

She dropped her skirt and leaned her face over him, rolling it a little so that he could see she was disgusted. "Well there then," she said. She shook the toy spider in her hand and then dropped it on his face.

He tried not to, he clenched his teeth and tried to keep it back, but the noiseless loud fear poured out of his mouth, moo after moo of it, pure craziness. He was so frightened he couldn't hear himself, and he heard Mina calling:

"Coke! Coke! Come in here right now. Come in here."

Before she had stopped shouting the watery blond boy came in. He didn't even look at Mina but simply put the heel of his boot on Peter's chest and ground his

143

foot round and round, pushing down hard. The blond boy pushed harder until Peter couldn't breathe any more, and he had to stop mooing. Then the boy squatted and sat on his chest, bouncing his weight up and down so that he couldn't get out his fear. He drummed his arms and legs, banging the chain links, rubbing them across the floor.

The blond boy began to slap his face first with one hand and then with the other. "What's my name?" he said.

"Coke."

He slapped him again and again. "What's the rest of it? What's my full name?"

Peter was cold with unknowing. He formed sounds but no name emerged from them.

"Come on, baby. Stick with it. What's my full name, now?" The slapping had got progressively harder.

"Coke Rymer," he said.

"That's my baby," the blond boy said in a soothing tone of voice. "That's a way to go." He stood up with the meaningless nonchalance he always had about him. "We'll get you a drink now, okay?" Without pausing for an answer he kicked Peter hard on the side of his neck. "That's a baby," he said.

He groaned at the kick, but after the first uttering of pain was out he subsided into the whimpering which finally became only a strained silent heaving of his chest. He kept looking up at Coke's liquescent blue gaze; his own eyes were charged with pain and fear but not with hate. He would never have any more hate.

144

Apparently satisfied, Coke Rymer knelt and began to unlock the chained cuffs at his wrists and ankles. He was still murmuring soothingly. "All right now, you're coming right along. You're going to do all right, honey, you're going to do all *right*." When he finished with the locks he handed the bunch of keys on the long chain to Mina. She dropped the chain loop over her head, tucked the keys into her cotton blouse and buttoned it up. She stood away from the two of them, her arms folded. Coke Rymer hoisted him to his feet and held him up until he seemed steady enough to stand by himself. He stood wavering, his head dropped almost to his chest and lolling back and forth; floundered across the room and leaned backward against the flimsy dinette table. He stroked carefully at his wrists; there were scarlet ichorous bands on them where the broad iron cuffs had rubbed the skin away. It made him feel very pitying to see his poor wrists like this.

"Huh," Mina said. "You ain't hurt. That's nothing."

"We'll get him a drink of liquor," Coke Rymer said. "That'll fix our little honeybunch up before you know it. Make a new man out of him." He swung open one of the rickety wall cupboard doors. Inside, it was full of empty bottles and broken glass. He brought down a pint bottle of murky stuff and shook it, looked at it against the broad light that streamed through the open door. "What'll you give me for this?" he said. He showed his dim little teeth in a stretched smile.

He could barely grunt. It sounded like gravel rattling in a box.

"Oh, go on and give it to him," Mina said. She watched him patiently, as if she was curious. Of course curiosity would never show in that locked face.

The boy held it out to him and he waited a wary moment to see if it would be jerked away. He got hold of it in both hands and then momentarily just stood clutching it out of fear of dropping or spilling it. He drank in short convulsive swallows. It tasted thick and mushy and warm, but it had a burning around the edges. As he lowered the bottle he lowered his head too and then again he stood clenching the bottle and, with the muscles of his chest, clenching his insides too. He had to keep it down, couldn't let it get away from him; he stood taut from his heels to his chin. After a long time the writhing spasms stopped. Again sweat came out on him all over.

Mina was still watching him. She spoke in an observing even tone: "They's chicken blood in that liquor."

He was still stuporous; her face was as blank to him as paper.

"You was the one done it yourself," she said. "You was the one pulled that chicken's head off and crammed that neck down in the bottle. I guess you didn't know it, but that's what you done. It was just last night." In the morning sunlight her eyes seemed paler than ever.

Coke Rymer sniggered.

He looked clumsily at the bottle in his hands, then put it carefully on the table. He was a long way past caring now. He stood still, waiting and dazed.

She stirred her feet and began talking to the blond boy. She had the full relaxed air of someone who has just seen a difficult juggling trick performed successfully. "Me and the girls has got to go off," she said. "I got to get me something to wear for tonight. You better keep your eye on him good while we're gone and see he gets this place cleaned up some. Don't let him drink too much of that liquor so he can't do nothing. You better get him something to eat at dinnertime too. We got to make him eat something."

His mind was clearing some. The narrow avenues of what he knew of his labors and his fear had emerged a little from the wet smoke. He understood that she was talking about him but that he didn't have to listen. And then he had to. She was telling him something. "Go on in there and wake them girls up," she said. "We got to get going."

"Wait a minute," Coke Rymer said. He turned to her. "I want to show him something." He came across to where Peter stood and spread his hand flat on the table, his fingers wide apart. "Look here," he said, "I want to show you something." He fetched a big folded knife from his pocket and let it roll in his hand. When he moved his thumb a sharp crying blade jumped from his fist, circled in the air. Peter moved back a little, trembling. The knife was Coke Rymer's man-thing, he didn't want it to hurt him; he didn't want to see it. Coke Rymer laid it on the table and twirled it around with his index finger. He was giggling. He picked the knife up at the end of the blade, pinching it with his thumb and forefinger. "Look at this," he said. He hesitated and then flipped the knife quickly upward. It spun round and round, a flashing pinwheel. When it came down the blade chucked into the tabletop in the space between the third and fourth fingers of Coke Rymer's left hand. He giggled. The knife quivered to stillness.

"That's enough of that stuff now," Mina said. "I want him to get some things done today. I don't want you messing around and playing with him all the time. He's got to get some things done."

Coke Rymer folded the knife and put it away. He turned toward her. "You want me to take away that ole pump handle?"

"I reckon not. You just quit deviling him and leave him alone. He's enough trouble the way he is already, without you picking at him."

"I wasn't hurting him none."

"Just leave him alone, I said." She spoke to Peter. "I thought I told you already to get them girls out of bed. I ain't got all day to fool around with you."

He slouched forward, going reluctantly toward the bedroom. He wanted her to make sure the yellow-haired boy wouldn't disturb the pump handle. She ought to stop him. The pump handle solaced him with its length and its fine heaviness in his hand; he loved to stroke along the long subtle curve of it; he liked just to have it near him, to hold it out before himself, admiring its blazing shininess and its heft. Hours and hours he had spent scrubbing and shining and oiling it. He knew that Mina derived a clear satisfaction from knowing that it was his man-thing, and he thought she ought not let Coke Rymer dally with it.—He couldn't understand the blond boy. There was nothing in him, nothing at all; he didn't understand why Mina tolerated him.

He lumbered through the narrow doorway into the living room. In here the light was dimmer and didn't bulge in his head so much. The torn shade was pulled almost down in the north window; little chinks and blocks of light shone in the holes. Through the west window he could see the squat cheap white frame house across the street, all yellow in the sunlight. One pillow lay staggered on the floor, dropped from the springs of the stained greasy wine-colored sofa across the room; along the top of the sofa back all the prickly nap had worn away. On the black little end table was the radio, which was on—the radio was always on—but now nobody had bothered to tune it to a station and it uttered only staccato driblets of static. There were a couple of broken cardboard boxes in one corner of the room, and a few sheets of newspaper were scattered on the floor. On the east wall beside the door were dime-store photographs of Marilyn Monroe, Jayne Mansfield and Elvis Presley, all dotted with flyshit. At the edge of the sofa and in two corners of the room were blurred remnants of the pattern which had once covered the dull rubbed linoleum.

The bedroom was to the south of the living room and he entered without knocking. A dark green shade covered the single bedroom window and in here it was much dimmer than in the living room. He had to wait until

149

his eyes adjusted to the darkness. Heaped together in the small bed in the corner—the big double bed on the left was Mina's—the girls stirred restlessly, sensing in their sleep Peter's presence in the room. He went to the bed, grasped a protruding pale shoulder and shook it as gently as he could. The startled flesh moved under his nerveless hand. "Whah." He shook her again and she mumbled some more and sat up. Because of the bad light her sharp face looked detached, a soft lantern. It was Bella. Her black hair came forward, hiding her face; she shook her head, raised her arms and stroked her hair back over her shoulders. Only her face and her breasts stood visible. Her breasts were like featureless faces; they bobbed softly as she fixed her hair. Enid shifted in her sleep, turning toward them, and flung her thin arm over Bella's gentle belly. She stopped manipulating her hair and for a moment stroked carefully the arm which lay on her.—He knew that this too was one of Mina's satisfactions, that Bella and Enid were after the woman in each other.—Then she tapped Enid's arm. "Sweetheart," she said, her voice thick and throaty from sleep, "wake up. Mina must want us to get up. Come on." Enid dug deeper into the bed.

Bella looked up at him, her gaze abstracted, visionless. Momentarily it seemed to him that there was something she wanted from him, and the thought frightened him. He stumbled back from the bedside.

"What do you think you're doing?" she said. Her voice was regaining its natural sharpness. "Go on away. Go get where you belong."

As he went out the door he saw Bella resume her loving ministering to Enid.

Mina was talking to Coke Rymer in the living room, and Peter went straight through and on through the kitchen out to the back porch. He wanted to check his pump handle, to see if it was still where he had hidden it—that was the one thing he could remember from the day before. The porch cracked and swayed under his footsteps, the boards weakening with rot or termites. A double handful of big blue-and-green flies was flocked on the carcass of the headless chicken that lay there. They skipped about on the queasy body, making a noise like muttered swearing. Already the air was hot, viscid, and the singing of the flies seemed to increase the oppressiveness of the heat. He nudged the chicken with his bare toe and the flies swirled up in a funnel-shaped pattern and then settled again immediately. With his forearm he wiped his mouth; he couldn't understand how he could do something like that. All the glare of the sun seemed focused on the murdered bird.

He stepped down into the fluffy dust of the back yard. The yard was small, and underneath the dust was burning packed clay. A ruptured hog-wire fence unevenly straggled the rectangular borders, and here and there long shoots of blackberry vine poked through. In the north corner of the yard was the little low weatherstained shed from which he averted his eyes without even thinking about it, with the strength of a habit enforced by sheer instinct. He went around the edge of the little porch, which was laid out at the back of the house like

151

a perfunctory throw rug, and peeked underneath, where the pile of daubed stones supported it. There, crosswise in a space between two joists, lay the pump handle. He hadn't realized until he found the handle that he'd been holding his breath and it came in a swoop out his mouth and nose, all too heavily redolent of what had happened to his insides. He wiped his mouth. He got the pump handle and stood and held it before him, hefting it warm and solid in his hand, beholding it in the sunlight. He examined it all over for a speck of rust or dirt, but it was clean and shiny as quicksilver.

"Well, so that's where you keep it then? Well, that's all I wanted to know."

He looked up. Coke Rymer was standing at the edge of the porch, leaning against the post support and whittling slowly at the edge of it. Dismayed, Peter stepped back.

Coke Rymer showed his meaningless grin; his teeth were little and yellow. "That's all in the world I needed to know, where you keep hiding that ole pump handle."

He stepped farther back, gingerly swinging the bright handle like a pendulum in front of his legs. He decided that if the watery blond boy got down into the yard after him he would hit him, he would make blood come. Already now he was whimpering.

The other folded his knife and returned it to his pocket. "Aw, hush up. I ain't going to hurt you." He grinned again. "You better come on in here now and get started on this stuff Mina wants you to get done. She's liable to get mad if you don't, and I guess you don't want her to get mad at you. You'd be a even more pitiful sight than you are if she was to get mad and get ahold of you."

Still he hung back, but he had stopped swinging the pump handle. He clasped it fondly across his belly.

Coke Rymer looked at him. "Aw, you can bring that old thing with you. What's it matter to me?" He turned and briskly went inside.

He shuffled unsteadily up the two creaky steps onto the porch. He didn't mind the work so much. He was just hoping they wouldn't make him eat the gooey soft-fried eggs and toast for lunch.

FIVE

It wasn't long until September. In another one of his
moments of clarity he sat inspecting his body. A good
view of it; they dressed him now in only these tattered
blue swimming trunks, no matter the weather. The
boards of the hated floor were sharp with cold in the
mornings, and sweated dirt streaked his body like paint.
On his lower shoulder were still pieces of the silvery
quarter-moon scars that Mina's teeth had left on him,
but now these were beginning to be lapped over by the
tattooing. Where he wasn't filthy dirty he was gaudy as
a comic book. They had begun at the base of his spine.
He had lain stretched on Mina's bed, grasping the iron
bars hard and weeping without control, while Coke
Rymer, nervous and sweating and cursing him, held the
nervous hot electric needle and Mina stood calmly
watching. "No, not there, you're not doing it right,"
she had said. "No, you're not doing it right." And then
she would lean over and touch softly the spot she wanted
decorated and Peter's body would jerk, as shocked as

154

if her cold finger were the burning needle again. "Yeah, yeah, I see," Coke Rymer would say, his voice querulous, whining asperity. "If I could just get this son of a bitch to hold still." The sweat dripped oily from his face onto Peter's back and then ran itching down his side. It was maddening. At the end of the first session they had got a couple of mirrors so that he could see the handiwork. He rose weakly from the bed, where the imprint of his body was wet and vehement. He looked where they directed and he couldn't help crying out, "Is that all? Is that all?" in anguish and impotent rage. In the mirrored mirror was his skin and on it only a small misshapen yellow circle, about the size of a quarter, with an indistinguishable dark head in it and letters—he supposed these marks were letters—in a tongue he had never seen. It was a coin on his spine, or the sun, sardonically injured. Was that all? The intolerable waiting and the nervous pain, just for that? —But now he had got used to it, it was no more than being swarmed over by a troop of red ants. They all took turns, Coke and Bella and Enid, but he wept no more under the needle, the artwork had come to seem necessary to him, and he was coolly curious as to how it would turn out. The little gold coin—or maybe it was a sun—had been obscured almost; in his mirrored skin he had to search hard to find this starting point in the crawly fantastic turf his back had become. On his back nothing was what it was, there were no demarcations, no outlines; nothing was formed, it was all in the process of becoming. Except here a large eye, marbled and fluid; there a crippled hand, the fingers webbed together with sperm. Scattered purple lumps which might be grapes, but pendent from nothing, not attached; knives which looked melting but still cruel; blue fernlike hair; smeared yellowish-white spots, which might be stars dripping down the soundless void, spots of startling silence on this raucous grating jungle, the polychrome verdure suggesting an impossible pointless fecundity and even the odor of this, but the whole impression transitory as dew. Here, was this an inky bird struggling into shape? Really, were these great fish? Or bared unjoined tendons? Was this a clot of spiny seaweed? . . . A worm? . . . And now lapping over his shoulder onto his chest, covering over the scars of Mina's bites, these looked like green licks of flame, upside-down.

In a muffled flimsy way Peter could share their clear pleasure in the work. It was Bella's turn now, and now that they laid him on his back to perform he observed the intense concentration in her bladelike face. She used the needle as carefully as if she were making a painful embroidery, and he felt obscurely flattered. When she worked on him she had about her none of the contemptuous stupor she used with the men that she and Enid brought to the house. But of course she had no interest in the men except for their money: a dark manner she had, and her body smelled always of earth, of the sandy dirt outside, beaten clangorous by the sun. Mina too was intent on the tattooing, though her face, forever closed, wouldn't show her interest. But Peter knew it was there, and felt a crazy gladness. Clearly he was being prepared, clearly he was being readied, although he didn't know for what. But that finally was unimportant to him. He guessed that his evening performances, which he could not remember, were growing in intensity and in absurdity, and that he was gradually fixing for some simple horrifying climax to it all; but he didn't care. The careful progress of the tattooing gave him the feeling of being new-made; his old self—perhaps his only self (that was all right too)—was being obliterated; it was almost as if he were being reborn, inch by inch, and this feeling was effervescent in him, sometimes buoyed him over his hard depressions and the moments when he let go and felt himself falling, falling, falling through the void shaft between all the atoms.

He was sitting on the tiny back porch, the pump handle near, and the early afternoon sunlight was on his chest like thick cotton. The air seemed sugary and the scores of heavy flies fumbled about in it. Enid came out of the house to sit beside him; hitched her skirt over her white thighs and let her legs dangle in the sunlight. He didn't squirm away. He wasn't afraid of Enid, felt even a sort of melting pity for her: she was nothing, she was airy, empty as air, and herself fearful. She was blond very much as Coke Rymer was blond, but she was thin and graceless, had no cruelty in her. But still, he had furtively to move his hand and touch the pump handle. There; he felt better.

Her voice was a singsong whisper. "I always have to

157

do like you do," she said. "I have to do whatever Bella tells me to, just like you have to do whatever Coke tells you to do. It's funny, the way it is."

Peter didn't answer. It hurt to talk; his throat had been stripped raw by the drinking.

Her legs flashed when she moved them in the light. "And Bella and Coke have to do what Mina wants them to. It's funny." She shrugged; her shoulders were thin as dry leaves. "But I don't care what they do, they can't do anything that would really bother me."

He almost spoke. He wanted to tell her that she just didn't know, that they could do things to her she couldn't imagine, she would have pain and humiliation she could never understand. And worse, she would be deprived the solace of her outrage, she would have none.

"I guess I'm next too," she said, "I know it. When you're all gone, I mean, when they're finished with you, they'll start on me. But I really don't care, because I've put up with just about everything already."

He dropped his head sadly. It was all too clear that she referred to his death. He wondered for an instant why she had been told, and why they had kept it from him, for surely his foreknowledge would be the most closely observed part of their treatment of him. But he discarded the thought: she had not been told, no; she knew about his death in the same way that he did, for he had known long ago, even before the death of Sheila. He corrected himself. Before he had murdered her. . . . But Enid was still mistaken; there were things in store which would pain her impossibly. She was made for a

158

victim too: empty and pliant as air, she had neither will nor way to strike back. Even so, he must admire her courage. She could guess something of what was coming, at least, and still she kept a resigned composure. Of course, any kind of courage was of no use without some allegiance to, some tenacity for, one's life, and Enid was void of these. To the end she would simply be what she was already, a ready-made victim. And perhaps it would be easier for her. He had sometimes thought that it would be much less painful for him if he could just resign himself, could just accept without struggle whatever black looming entry they'd shove him through next. . . . And a darker thought rose to the surface: he wondered if Enid was being set as an example to him by Mina. Was her acquiescence, for all its show of courage, one of the final temptations for him? Were they trying finally to rupture in him a last thin shard of integrity, an integrity which must disturb Mina but which he could not himself discover? Or was this thought a single piece of self-flattery? The doubt in his mind was like a hard iron ring and, as ever, he hefted up his shiny pump handle for some kind of affirmation. And now it was not enough. Self-pity welled in his heart like empty tears to the eye. The pump handle too, like every other object, like everything but his tough chains and the boards of the floor and the quivery tattooing needle, was losing its presence. It lacked its former heft, its authority. It was going away from him; now he was going to be entirely alone.

Enid pushed lightly off the edge of the porch and went

round in front of him up the steps into the house. He
listened to the whisper of her bare feet on the wood,
over the linoleum. And he heard Bella's sharp voice
accost the blond girl as she entered the living room.
"Here's Enid now, and she's a pretty thing, isn't she?"
A piercing voice, a throaty male tenor, Bella's. "You
ought to put some meat on your bones, honey," she said.
"You're just a bag of bones. I still love you, though,
because you're so blond. I always was crazy about
blonds. You'd be just about perfect, I think, if you'd
just put some meat on those bones." She was silent for
a moment, and Peter could picture the scene: Bella was
sitting in the balding sofa in her long brown dress, her
legs crossed like a man's, ankle laid across knee, exposing her long stale dusty thighs; and now she stubbed
out her cigarette with a single jab of her wrist, sharp.
"Come here," he heard her say. "Come here to mama."

He sighed. The afternoon was blazing away; the sun
had dipped lower, but the light was still white, still
hot. It didn't seem the sun had moved, but that the
landscape had ached upward after it, as if the heat that
had soaked through the dust into the pressed earth was
not enough, would never be enough. In the center of the
world was a fast deep iciness, pure recalcitrant cold,
which could absorb the whole heat of the sun and every
point of light; yearned after it. This coldness impinged
upon him; he had felt its approach and now he felt it
so imposing that his body shivered, anticipated.—The
hand of every natural thing was turned against him,

he knew it. The pump handle felt light as balsa wood, bodiless. There was no point at which his body was in contact with the world; his body garish, he floated a garish emptiness.

But something with a weight was dipping into his shoulder. He looked. Coke Rymer's hand upon him, and he rose as steadily as he could, not wanting the boy cruelly to help him to his feet. But he lurched into him—it was almost impossible for him to keep his feet any more—and Coke Rymer shoved him sharply backward and smacked his left jaw with a sharp elbow. "Goddam you," the boy said. "By God, I'll learn you." He slapped him across the eyes and then took his hand and led him inside.

His vision was dazed with tears. Something in his head bored like a big auger.

Coke Rymer leaned him against the spotted kitchen wall, the way one might prop a board up while he turned to something else. The blond boy stepped back to look at him, but even in his mean eyes most of the cruel interest was gone. This handling of him was routine, and the performance was much too far along for the routine to carry interest. Now all was bent toward acceleration, toward the meaty ending.

"Well, honeybunch, can I give you a drink?"

Coke Rymer's figure swam blurry before him; he tried to fix it tight, but couldn't. He shook his head. He couldn't drink any more. His body would no longer accept the stuff; he couldn't keep it down and there was no comfort in it.

161

"You sure now, sweetheart? Used to be, you'd hanker after a drink some."

He kept mute and still.

"Well, okay then, whatever you say. Come on in here."

He led—half carried—Peter into the darkened bedroom, and Peter fell almost gratefully into Mina's wide bed. Voluntarily he grasped the bars of the bedhead, readying himself for the tattooing session. It was Coke's turn once more; Mina stood away, slightly behind him, ready to supervise. Bella turned on the naked overhead bulb, and the room went stark and shadowless. Peter gazed down at his long body with clinical interest. He hadn't imagined that his thin being could grow so much thinner; he was all angles and knobs. His ribs were distressingly evident, stiff, stiff as fingers of the dead. When he breathed his skin seemed to move reluctantly over his ribs, he could almost hear a susurration. Ah, poor body, with its single destination, powerless and expectant. Coke Rymer reached to a cord at Peter's navel, snapped it loose, began to maneuver the tattered bathing trunks from his waist.

He squirmed and croaked.

"Now don't start that goddam meowling," Mina said. "You just hush up. Because they ain't nothing you can do about it anyhow."

Only disjointed croaks he could muster from his throat.

"Hush. They ain't nothing there that could hardly

get hurt, is there? You ain't got nothing down there to be touchous about. Just you keep quiet."

The bare bedroom was filling with men. They jostled together, unreal, tough-looking; they wore sport shirts or white shirts open at the collar. He couldn't count them, the light from the big bulb jabbed his eyes. He thought that he recognized some of them; they were customers, the men the whores brought in. They had red faces, baked, hoodlums from the town of Gordon, scoured, God knew how, out of the beer joints and hamburger joints, and brought here for the spectacle. They didn't speak; they were silent except for an occasional single whisper and an accompanying titter.

Coke Rymer gave a final tug and the swim trunks came off his feet. "There, by God," the blond boy said. Peter watched him; he was trembling and sweating. He was more fearful than Peter, and somehow it made sense. Coke still had to fear Mina, but Peter didn't any longer. No matter what happened to him, he was well out of that. It was a strange funny thought, but when he laughed he uttered only a scraping gurgling sound.

"Hush up," Mina said. "I ain't going to tell you no more."

He clenched his teeth, he could hear the unnerving rub of them together; he was going to keep silent, not from fear of Mina but in the hope of frustrating Coke Rymer. He knew that Coke hoped for his pained re- actions, that they were a great part of what he had now to subsist upon. He too was losing grip. After she was

163

finished with Peter and with Enid, it would be Coke's turn. Peter began to wish that he could see it, he would like to know how Coke would bear up under what Mina had planned for him. Whatever it was, it would be different from Peter's treatment; and he guessed that it would be worse. Abruptly he felt a queer sympathy for the boy, who was pushing forward now through the ring of strangers, bearing the black-handled needle with its black cord dangling; abruptly he was glad that he wouldn't have to watch the spectacle of Coke Rymer's going. As the blond boy squatted by the bedhead, grunting, to plug in the electric needle Peter glanced at the top of his sticky hair. He felt that he almost smelled the bad nerves in him. It was a performance for Coke as well as for Peter.

He held the bars of the bedhead as tightly as he could, as Coke Rymer stood above him, leaning forward in a sort of triumphant uncertainty. But those bars seemed to go away from his grip; like the pump handle they had lost substance. In all the world there was nothing in which he could touch, find his maleness; all drifted.

Mina came closer. She was ready to begin. She put the tip of her index finger on her cold tongue and leaned and touched Peter's chest just below the right nipple. "There," she said. "You can start right there."

Coke turned about and sat on the edge of the bed, pressing it so that Peter slid slightly against him. "Scoot your ass over," Coke said. His voice had become the uncertain liquid falsetto once more. Peter shifted. Coke leaned sidewise over him; he was already sweating heavily and the oily drops fell from his forehead onto Peter's belly, trickled into his navel.

He held on as tight as he could and kept silent as long as he could. From the circle of the strangers came an occasional restless unsurprised mutter. . . . Perhaps they had expected more from him; he was being too quiet to please them, and he didn't want to please them. But in a while he was muttering hoarsely; they all peered at him more closely. He couldn't see very well what Coke was up to with the needle; it hurt his neck to look because of the way he had to crane. There was a murky green-and-purple band filling in from right to left across his chest, joining the place where the tattooing had already lapped over his shoulder. Around the tattooing the bare skin was flushed, heated, swollen; the design, if it could be called a design, appeared on him like a great lurid continent thrusting itself out of the sea. The upper part of his chest was numb, but it afforded him no real relief. He had ceased muttering, though. The only sounds now were the intense breathing of the five or six men gathered about and the warm steady hum of the electric needle, like the flight of a hornet near away in summer air. Not enough was happening; he felt Mina's boredom, and he wasn't surprised when she wet her finger and placed it high on his left cheek, not far below his eye.

"There," she said. "Start there again."

Coke Rymer held the needle above Peter's neck and

165

turned to look at her. "How come you want me to start up there now?" he said. "Ain't I done enough work for one day?" His voice, the watery feminine whine.

"Work; you don't know what it means, work. You don't know what the word is. You go ahead now, like I showed you."

He turned back to Peter. His hand was shaking savagely. For the first time Peter felt that he saw in those wet blue eyes an attitude toward himself that was not indifferent, nor fearful, nor contemptuous, but almost fellowly, almost sympathetic. And this discovery was more frightening than any other. If this sort of feeling could be roused in Coke Rymer, it meant that the edge really was close, was nearing steadily.

"Here we go then, sweetheart," Coke said. "Hold on to your hat."

At the first prick of the needle he jerked his head aside, sputtered with stifling pain. Enid was standing at the foot of the bed, and through his pinched eyes he saw that her mouth was working, rounding and widening on breaths of air, though she made no sound. She had in her eyes a full wasted pity. He thought that she had better keep it for herself, Mina was killing two birds with one stone.

Coke grasped him harshly with his left hand under his chin; his fingers were tight on the spit glands under his ears. "Goddam your eyes," he said. "Hold your head still."

He acquiesced in his mind; he wanted as little trouble as possible, he wanted it to be over soon.

166

But when the needle was at his cheek again, his head recoiled. He couldn't help it. Now his body was taut with apprehension, and warm liquid streamed down his face, across his mouth. Taste of salt. When his head moved, the needle must have ripped his cheek. He looked at Coke in despair. He had made him angry, he hadn't wanted to. It would be easy for the boy enraged to plunge the vibrant needle into his eye.

But Coke turned away, turned toward Mina. "I ain't going to do it no more," he said. "I'm tired of it. You can do it your goddam self."

She didn't smile, but her voice was levelly humorous. "All right. That's fine. I guess you've had a hard day and I feel real sorry for you. You give Bella that needle and then you can go and lie down and take a little rest." In the blazing room she was the only cool thing. "I'll be around and tend to you in just a little while."

Bella poked her way through the waiting unreal circle of men. "Give me the needle," she said. "I never have believed that you had the guts of a weasel. . . . Isn't it true that he shamed him in a fight once?" She asked the question of Mina. "Isn't that true? That Coke was afraid of something like *him?*" She gestured toward Peter with the needle she had taken from the blond boy. It was still running, humming.

Coke rose from the bed and pushed his way clumsily through the group. He rubbed his streaming face. Mina took his place on the edge of the bed, a neat aggressive motion.

"I won't be able to do it, I can't hold it still," Peter said. But the words became mere grating gasps, formed from pain and fear.

Mina surveyed him from the foot of the bed. There seemed clear in her steady eyes the knowledge of what he was saying. "That's all right, honey," she said to Peter. "Don't you worry about a thing. We'll take care of you fine." She touched two of the near men in the circle and they looked at her, waiting, shamefully scared. "Take hold of his feet," she said. "Hold him down good and tight."

They grasped Peter's ankles, unhesitating; pressed them so hard into the lumpy mattress that he had to let go the bars of the bedhead. His forearms were prickly with exhaustion, his wrists felt all injured tendon, his palms were bruised scarlet.

"You-all grab his hands too. We got to stop him from jumping all over the place."

One of the men, fantastic and red-faced as the others, took Peter's right hand, bent his elbow hard, bringing his forearm under his neck, and then took both wrists together, one atop the other; held them crossed hard with his knee. His face was unreadable. He steadied his stance by holding to the bedhead.

Bella took Coke's place at the bed edge. She took Peter's chin with thumb and finger and turned the torn cheek toward her. "Look at that," she said. "Coke's made a mess of this, it's just a mess."

"You can let that part go then," Mina said. "You'll have to start lower down." She wet her finger, leaned

168

over the foot of the bed, touched him where it would be most sexually excruciating; but there was no longer sexuality in him. She straightened, her eyes still plainly bored; and from the strangers a murmur of . . . Was it satisfaction? They were expectant.

He nodded. It was as he had thought; there was no way out of Mina's thinking. He came at last to anticipate her every maneuver, horrified because she had so usurped his mind. It was his own head that labored so to produce his own humiliation.

Bella rose and moved lower on the bed.

The moos were on him, implacable, but now they didn't care; they let him sound away, absorbed in their work. He kept passing out and rousing again to consciousness. The world was flaring brightly before him; gasping and flickering down again. It was the most fragile tendril that held him tied to it all.

At last they brought him back again for the final time. Coke Rymer had returned, and he helped one of the strangers hoist Peter to his feet. They almost dropped him; he had no control.

"That's all, sweetie," Coke said. "That's all there is."

Mina came forward and looked him over. They held him pinioned by arms and shoulders. He couldn't see her well, he didn't look at her face, but felt the cold wash of her gaze on all his body. "Wouldn't you like to see how it turned out?" she said. "I believe you've improved a whole lot." She spoke to Coke and the other. "Bring him over here in front of the mirror."

They dragged him standing before the wardrobe. He saw the image; nodded wisely. His legs were still naked, untouched by the needle, but they were no longer his, no longer even supported his body. They looked irrelevant and alien, detachable. The remainder of his body was obliterated; it had been absorbed entirely into another manner of existence, a lurid placeless universe where all order was enlarged bitter parody. Even his bare skin where the needle had not tracked was a part of it all, and the bloodstain over his face was integral, was assuredly important. His body now was a river, was flowing away. He nodded again.

"Well now," Mina said, "I'm glad to see that you like it. I think it does you a lot of good myself." She spoke to Coke Rymer and the other man. "Well, take him out there where I told you to."

Immediately they began dragging him toward the door. The line of strangers fell away and they went through into the living room, turned, went through the kitchen. It was dark and no cooler. The stars looked close and hot, and in the darkness were clumps of darker shadow. He breathed deep, convulsively; he felt almost as if he had been holding his breath for hours. No, but in the air he had been breathing had been no sustenance for his lungs. The porch floor creaked as they shuffled across it; the board steps cried out. He was not resisting, but he couldn't aid them, either. There was nothing left in his body. He had no body.

Shuffling in the thick dust they took him across the

barren ground. He gazed upward and the sky looked narrow and vile, hurrying against him. They were taking him, he knew it, to the low weather-stained shed. There the god permitted his being at times to obtrude into perception. He had feared the obscure shed and the altar with all his deep and fearful hate, but now he was hopeful for it. He wished that he could move toward it under his own volition. Coke Rymer unlatched the shabby raspy door and they flung him in. He fell on his back, and for a few minutes lay still. He knew that they wouldn't come in to help him sit up; they wouldn't enter at all. Coke Rymer gazed at him through the door only for a moment; threw him—it was like throwing a foul scrap of meat to a dog—a limp mock salute. "Well, bye-bye sweetheart," he said. "I guess I won't be seeing you for a while. Might be a good long time." He turned and followed the other man, both forms dissolving into shadowed night. They left the door open, dark gray rectangle scratched with the wiry lines of blackberry vines. He heard Mina coming; and he pushed himself backward through the dirt floor littered with wads of paper and corncobs.

She leaned forward in the low door, putting her hands at the top to hold herself. "Well, there you are now," she said. "You look like you're comfortable. You look like you're going to be all right. You're all right, ain't you?"

He couldn't answer.

"Well, you look all right to me. I'll just leave you here and I'll be back in a little while."

All he could make out of her was her luminous gray eyes, spots in the darkness. He nodded, he was sure she could see him.

"Yeah, I knew you knew I'd be back." She laughed, a slight dry sound, humorless. She stepped back; shut the door lightly; shot the solid latch forward.

He waited. He heard her going away, and then he heard nothing for a long while. Then, a faint rustling in a far corner: a rat, perhaps. And then again silence, disturbed by his own unsteady breathing. Inside his chest it was as painful as outside. In here it was inky dark and his eyes did not grow accustomed to it. He could barely make out the shape of the silly altar, loose boards of uneven lengths laid over two rickety sawhorses. Very gradually his breathing grew in volume, stertorous, bladed in the throat. It grew and grew; he could feel the passage of it on his skin. It was not his breathing. He understood. He opened his mouth to breathe. The galaxies poured down his throat, thick tasteless dust he could not spit out, could not vomit. The breathing was icy on his skin; impression of swift wind continually on him, but the dust of the floor not stirring. Slowly he raised his hands to rub his face. It was cold and dry and felt not like flesh, but like wood or leather. It was himself no longer. . . . Point of vague light somewhere in the air, but then not light: a circle of blackness, a funnel that sucked all the light away, even the light of his body which was glowing with a faint phosphorescent pulse. He looked into his body,

172

looked through it: wide clots of dust, a thin winking membrane where the nebulae were being born. . . . Something solid out there. An angleless wall without protuberance; no, not solid; a bending wall, breathing upon him.

Eye.

Tooth.

Glimpsed and then erased, wiped coolly from vision. The god Dagon assumed the altar.

Reptilian. Legless. Truncated scaly wings, flightless, useless. The god Dagon was less than three feet long. Fat and rounded, like the belly of a crocodile. He couldn't see the mouth hidden away under the body, but he knew it: a wirelike grin like a rattlesnake's; double rows of venomous needles in the maw. On this side a nictitating eye, but he thought that on the other side there would be no eye, but merely a filmy blind spot, an instrument to peer into the marrow of things. The visible eye gray, almost white. A body grayish-pink like powdery ashes. Chipped and broken scales covered it, tightly overlapped. It breathed and this took a long time. The froglike belly distended, contracted.—The reptilian shape was immobile; there was no way for it to move upon the earth.

He recognized the god Dagon.

An idiot. The god was omnipotent but did not possess intelligence. Dagon embodied a naked will uncontrollable. The omnipotent god was merely stupid.

Peter laughed, his teeth shone in the dark.

He confronted the god. The presence of Dagon displaced time, as a stone displaces water in a dish. Surely hours elapsed in the stare that was between them.

Merely a ruptured idiot stubby reptile.

The god Dagon went away. Suddenly winked out; whisked.

At last Peter relaxed. He smiled in the dark. He had faced the incomprehensible manifestation and he still maintained himself; he was still Peter Leland. He blinked his eyes gratefully, casually turned his head from the altar. He heard Mina coming and turned to face the door, still smiling in the dark, uncaring and relaxed. She opened the flimsy door and entered without hesitation. In her right hand she bore Coke Rymer's man-thing, faintly gleaming. She took a handful of his hair in her left hand and Peter knelt forward on his knees and raised his head. Happily he bared his throat for the knife.

SIX

Peter Leland died and came through death to a new mode of existence. He did not forget his former life, and now he understood it. The new vantage point of his psyche was an undefined bright space from which he could look back upon this little spot of earth and there see the shape of his life in terms not bitterly limited by misery and fear. At his death he did not relinquish the triumphant grasp of his identity he had acquired in encountering Dagon face to face. He had come through. In this surrounding brightness there was no time, and he watched his career unfold itself again and again beneath him and he laughed, without rancor and without regret. Now his whole personality was a benevolent clinical detachment.

He understood suffering now and the purpose of suffering. In an almost totally insentient cosmos only human feeling is interesting or relevant to what the soul searches for. There is nothing else salient in the whole tract of limitless time, and suffering is simply one means of carving a design upon an area of time, of charging with human meaning each separate moment of time. Suffering is the most expensive of human feelings, but it is the most intense and most precious of them, because suffering most efficiently humanizes the unfeeling universe. Not merely the shape of his own life taught him this, but the history of all lives, for from here he perceived with a dispassionate humor the whole of human destiny.

Metaphor amused him—and this was necessary, for in this place metaphor was a part of substance. Here he had no properly physical form apart from metaphor. And now it seemed his task to find and take his likeness in every possible form in the universe; he was to become a kind of catalogue of physical existence and of the gods. There were metaphors for everything: sometimes all his past life appeared to him in the image of a gleaming snail track over a damp garden walk; or a black iron cube, two inches square; or a shred of discolored cuticle; or a frayed shoelace.

No regret and no anger in him, no nostalgia for the painful limits he had metamorphosed out of. He was filled with an unrepressed motiveless benevolence. He contemplated with joy the unity of himself and what surrounded him. He deliberated what form his self should take now, thinking in a tuneless dreaming fashion of every possible guise. Galactic ages must have passed before he finally gave over and took the form of Leviathan. Peter took the form of the great fish, a glowing shape some scores of light-years in length. He was filled with calm; and joyfully bellowing, he wallowed and sported upon the rich darkness that flows between the stars.

$\mathcal{V}$oices of the $\mathcal{S}$outh

Hamilton Basso
 *The View from Pompey's
  Head*
Richard Bausch
 Real Presence
 Take Me Back
Robert Bausch
 On the Way Home
Doris Betts
 *The Astronomer and
  Other Stories*
 *The Gentle Insurrection
  and Other Stories*
Sheila Bosworth
 Almost Innocent
 Slow Poison
David Bottoms
 Easter Weekend
Erskine Caldwell
 Poor Fool
Fred Chappell
 Dagon
 The Gaudy Place
 The Inkling
 It Is Time, Lord
Kelly Cherry
 Augusta Played
Vicki Covington
 Bird of Paradise
R. H. W. Dillard
 The Book of Changes
Ellen Douglas
 A Family's Affairs
 A Lifetime Burning
 The Rock Cried Out
 Where the Dreams Cross
Percival Everett
 Cutting Lisa
 Suder
Peter Feibleman
 *The Daughters of
  Necessity*
 A Place Without Twilight

William Price Fox
 Dixiana Moon
George Garrett
 An Evening Performance
 Do, Lord, Remember Me
 The Finished Man
Ellen Gilchrist
 The Annunciation
Marianne Gingher
 Bobby Rex's Greatest Hit
Shirley Ann Grau
 The Hard Blue Sky
 *The House on Coliseum
  Street*
 The Keepers of the House
Ben Greer
 Slammer
Barry Hannah
 The Tennis Handsome
Donald Hays
 The Dixie Association
William Humphrey
 Home from the Hill
 The Ordways
Mac Hyman
 No Time For Sergeants
Madison Jones
 A Cry of Absence
Nancy Lemann
 Lives of the Saints
 Sportsman's Paradise
Beverly Lowry
 Come Back, Lolly Ray
Valerie Martin
 A Recent Martyr
 Set in Motion
Willie Morris
 *The Last of the Southern
  Girls*
Louis D. Rubin, Jr.
 The Golden Weather

Evelyn Scott
 The Wave
Lee Smith
 *The Last Day the Dog-
  bushes Bloomed*
Elizabeth Spencer
 The Night Travellers
 The Salt Line
 This Crooked Way
 *The Voice at the Back
  Door*
Max Steele
 Debby
Virgil Suárez
 Latin Jazz
Walter Sullivan
 The Long, Long Love
Allen Tate
 The Fathers
Peter Taylor
 The Widows of Thornton
Robert Penn Warren
 Band of Angels
 Brother to Dragons
 World Enough and Time
Walter White
 Flight
James Wilcox
 *Miss Undine's Living
  Room*
 North Gladiola
Joan Williams
 *The Morning and the
  Evening*
 The Wintering
Christine Wiltz
 Glass House
Thomas Wolfe
 The Hills Beyond
 The Web and the Rock